Other
Sammy and Brian Mysteries
by Ken Munro

The Quilted Message
The Bird in the Hand
Amish Justice
Jonathan's Journal
Doom Buggy
Fright Train
Creep Frog
The Number Game
The Tin Box
The Toy Factory
The Medallion's Secret
Secret Under the Floorboard
The Mysterious Guest House
Fire, Smoke, and Secrets
Fireball
Grandfather's Secret
The Mysterious Baseball Scorecard
The Cross Keys Caper
The Buggy Heist

The Sammy and Brian Mysteries are available at special quantity discounts for sales promotion, fund-raisers, or educational uses. For details, write to:

Gaslight Publishers
1916 Barton Drive
Lancaster, PA 17603

Email: kemunro@comcast.net

The Indian Bones' Revenge

A Sammy & Brian Mystery #20

By Ken Munro

GASLIGHT PUBLISHERS

The Indian Bones' Revenge

Copyright © 2008
by Ken Munro

All rights reserved.

No part of this book may be reproduced or transmitted in any form or by any means, electronic or mechanical, including photocopy, recording, or any information storage or retrieval system, without the express written permission of the publisher, except where permitted by law.
This book is a work of fiction. Most characters and events portrayed in this book are entirely fictional.

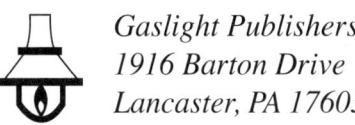

Gaslight Publishers
1916 Barton Drive
Lancaster, PA 17603

Email: kemunro@comcast.net

Library of Congress Number: 2008933980
International Standard Book Number: 978-1-60126-128-1

Printed 2008 by
Masthof Press
219 Mill Road
Morgantown, PA 19543-9516

Dedication

To Mary Elisabeth Swift Seibert,
my granddaughter.

To all the construction workers who
put their lives in danger
every working day.

Special thanks to:

*Jim Hagelgans
Peter Seibert
Alison Mallin
Ron Munro
Gene Hansen
Tracy Palmer*

Chapter One

The track hoe's bucket clawed at the dirt, opening a foundation suitable for the new convention center. The excavator swung around and again shook its contents into the dump truck. Several more scoopfuls and the truck would pull away well fed.

The next claw swoop was suddenly halted when Harry Hoover, the foreman, waved his arms and shouted, "Stop! Stop!"

Tom Boyer rammed his head out the cab window. "What's up? Did I hit another pipeline?"

"Just come over here and take a look at this."

Tom Boyer left his seat and swung down to the ground. He adjusted his hard hat and glanced at where his boss was pointing. This time the newly dredged-up debris contained more than dirt and stone.

"Oh, man, this is not good," Harry Hoover said, as he stooped and shook dirt from several bone-like objects.

Before Tom could respond to the new discovery, a middle-aged woman hurried toward them. Harry recognized her as a frequent visitor to the construction site. "Lady, you're not allowed in here," he said, standing between her and the bucket.

She nodded. "Those might be Indian bones. Indians lived in the area you know."

"How can you be sure they're even bones?" Harry asked without moving aside.

She tapped her thigh. "The long one is a femur bone. I know bones."

"They're just bits of old wooden sticks," Harry said. He grabbed the woman's arm and rushed her back up the dirt incline to the sidewalk.

When Harry returned, Tom said, "You were a little rough on her, weren't you? She was just trying to be helpful."

"Are you crazy? Don't you realize what's happening here?" Harry said, moving closer to his friend and looking around. "If these are any kind of human bones and word gets out, this construction site will be shut down for 30 to 90 days."

"But if they are human bones, we have to report this, Harry. That's the law."

Harry moved in closer. "You're not thinking. Who's our boss?"

"Stan Lowe," Tom said.

"Right. Stan Lowe of Lowe Construction. And who has a bucketful of money invested in the Lancaster County Convention Center?"

Tom shrugged. "Okay, so Stan has his life savings and a mortgage on his house in this project. So what? That's a chance he takes."

"It's not only him, Tom. It's us. Can you afford to be out of work for three months or more? If Lowe Construction goes bankrupt, we'll be fired."

Tom recoiled back. He glanced around the site. The dump truck driver was in his cab drinking coffee and listening to the radio, waiting for that last scoop of dirt. The other workers were elsewhere, applying their trade and working on a time schedule. The convention center was to open that next April.

"So we're to forget about the bones. Is that it, Harry?"

"That's right," Harry said and backed up and knelt in the dirt with his back to any spectators who might be watching. His hands shuffled around clods of dirt and came up empty. "There are only two bones here, Tom. Probably animal bones."

Tom Boyer took his hard hat off and rubbed his sleeve over his face. He had to think. He stepped closer to the bucket and pointed. "Is that all? Only two bones?"

Harry lifted a clump of dirt and shook it. "That's it."

"Then why are they there?"

"Do you know what we have, Tom? Years ago some girl's dog died, and the parents buried it here."

Tom shook his head. "We won't get away with it, Harry. I'm starting to feel creepy already."

Harry formed his hands into a scoop and took his time sifting through the remaining clods of dirt. Finding no more bones or relics, he looked up at Tom. "See? There's nothing else here."

Tom turned and thought about all the construction workers who would be out of work. He shook his head and faced Harry. "If we ignore this, I don't know if I can live with it. This could be trouble."

"If we keep our mouths shut, what's the problem?" Harry added. "Nobody can prove anything. We ditch this stuff, and the problem goes away. We keep our jobs, construction goes on, the convention center meets its deadline, and Stan Lowe makes a pile of money. Everyone wins."

Tom watched as his friend stuffed the bones under his shirt. "What about the woman?" Tom asked. "She saw the bones."

Harry looked up. "What bones?" He stood, pressing an arm against his shirt. "All she saw were two pieces of wood that she thought were bones." Before Tom could answer, Harry added, "I'm going to the car to get my lunch pail. You better dump this load into the truck before the driver falls asleep."

As Harry walked away, Tom climbed back into the cab of the track hoe and looked beyond the dirt incline to the sidewalk.

The woman was still there, watching.

So was a man with a camera.

Chapter Two

Two months later

The month of June brought with it an influx of tourists to the Lancaster County area. School was out, and families were starting their vacations. The question this year was, would the high gas prices prevent people from traveling? To ease the pain, hotels and motels were offering free gas to customers.

Bird-in-Hand's super sleuth, fifteen-year-old Sammy Wilson, had other things on his mind as he headed home from the Farmer's Market. Without his partner, Brian, eating a hotdog with sauerkraut on the side at Brenda's Lunch Counter, just wasn't the same. He yearned for the "good times" with his best friend. Since Brian Helm and his family moved away over a month ago, Sammy had changed. He slowed down. As Brian would say, "Sammy, your get-up-and-go has got up and went."

Brian's attempt at humor made Sammy mad at times. Brian was naïve. He did and said things that made Sammy shudder. Brian created his own "reality" and became anyone he wanted to be. But above all, it was Brian's innocence that made him lovable and Sammy's best friend.

As Sammy drew nearer to the Bird-in-Hand Country Store run by his parents, his mother stepped outside the shop. "Sammy, a man came to talk to you." She pointed to the frame house next to the shop. "He's up in your bedroom."

Sammy sighed. He had mixed feelings. He relished the challenge of working a new case, but not by himself. Solving crimes without Brian seemed a lopsided affair. He frowned and hurried in through the side door to the kitchen.

Sammy's father was eating lunch at the table. He lowered his coffee cup and said, "You came back just in time."

"Mom said there's a man upstairs to see me. Is he still there?"

"I believe so."

The young detective hurried up the steps and into his bedroom. The room was semi-dark. The window blind was down, and the curtains drawn shut. He took another step and panned the room. He saw familiar shapes: the built-in bookcase, bulletin board, desk, and his bed.

The bed. Something or someone was lying there. Still. No movement.

Sammy moved closer to the strange form and bent over.

It was a body with the face pointed upward, the eyes closed.

As Sammy leaned in, the eyes popped open, causing the teen to jump back.

"Hi, Sammy. What's up?" came a familiar voice from the lifeless form.

Mr. Wilson stood by the door and snapped on the light. "Surprise!" he said and then retreated down the steps.

In seconds, Sammy saw and understood the staged affair.

It was Brian Helm who lay across the bed, his eyes fixed on the ceiling.

Sammy, recovering from the shock, staggered to his desk and crossed his arms across his chest. As if nothing had happened in the last month, he said, "You were to be here at 9 o'clock for our brainstorming session. Why are you two months late?" Sammy tried, but he couldn't put up the pretense any longer. With tears in his eyes, he rushed to the bed, and the boys wrestled until they ended up on the floor.

"I still got it. Right, Sammy?" Brian said, sitting on Sammy and pinning his arms to the floor.

Sammy lifted his head. "What are you doing here? You're supposed to be in California."

"We're back. I think my father got cold feet."

"What does that mean? He didn't like California?"

Brian shrugged, pushed himself off of Sammy, and sat up on the bed. "I think it had something to do with his job."

Sammy grabbed the edge of his desk and pulled himself up. He tried to make sense out of Brian's simple statement. He said, "Your father was promoted and transferred to the law firm's home office. He would have to take the California bar exam to practice law there. Maybe moving into a new area and having new responsibilities was too much to handle."

The bed squeaked as Brian bounced up and down. "I think it started when I got into trouble. But it wasn't my fault. The woman dropped the charges."

Sammy half-sat on the edge of his desk. "What was that all about? You mentioned it in an e-mail. Something about you buying a camera from a man, and you found a purse, and a woman said you stole it."

"Yeah, all I did was go into this Borders Bookstore out there in Oakland. A man asked me if I wanted to buy his camera so he could buy a book. The price was cheap, so I bought it. When I went outside the store, a purse was on the sidewalk, so I picked it up. Out of nowhere, this woman appeared with a policeman and said I snatched her purse from her. She said the camera I had in my hand had been in her purse."

"When I read your e-mail, I assumed the man who sold you the woman's camera was the person who stole her purse."

"Right. So after my father got me out of jail, I staked out the bookstore, but the man never came back."

Sammy rounded his desk, sat in his chair, and leaned back. "Do you see what's wrong here, Brian?"

"Yeah, I didn't do it. I was falsely accused. Right, Sammy?"

"Why did the woman accuse you in the first place?"

"Because she saw me with her purse and her camera in my hands."

"And yet her purse was grabbed from her."

"That's what she said."

Sammy spread his arms wide. "So she saw the person who took it."

"She said she did."

"Do you look anything like the man who sold you the camera?"

"I hope not. He was big and ugly."

"Do you see the problem, Brian?"

Brian's face lit up. "Yeah, why would she identify me as the thief if I wasn't the one she saw taking her purse?"

Sammy nodded. "Did you say she later dropped the charges?"

"Yeah, but my father still wasn't happy about it. In fact, it made him madder."

While thinking about what Brian said, Sammy got up and went to the window. He opened the curtains and raised the blind. "And after the charges were dropped, your father decided to return to Lancaster County," he said.

Brian smiled. "Yep."

"Maybe your father used your episode with the police as an excuse to come back."

Brian shrugged and said, "It could be."

"Or, maybe the purse snatching was staged to force your father to return."

"Who would do that? Why would they do that?"

"Maybe it was someone who wanted your father's job. Do you know if your father received any strange phone calls or e-mail messages at that time?"

Brian pulled a knee up and sat sideways on the bed. "I know he got one call that upset him, but he didn't talk about it."

"Is your father back here with the same law firm?"

"No, he's going to open his own office."

"Where are you living now? Do you have a house?"

"We're with my Aunt Catherine until we get a place. Our stuff is in storage. Everything's a mess. Right now, it's like living out of a motel room."

Sammy went to the bed. He faked a right jab to Brian's stomach. "Brian, you've changed. You lost weight," he said.

Brian stood from the bed. "It's the California air. It doesn't have the fat that Lancaster County air has."

The boys hugged. It came naturally, nothing to be ashamed about.

"I'm glad you're back," Sammy said.

"Me, too," Brian said, wiping away tears.

Mr. Wilson stuck his head in the door. "Now that the reunion is over, I just heard that Tom Boyer, our neighbor, is in the hospital. Do you want to come with me to see him? Your mother will stay in the store."

"What happened to him?" Sammy asked with concern.

"It happened yesterday. They found him confused and beat up, wandering down a back road."

"Brian, Tom operates the heavy, earth-moving machines on construction sites," Sammy said. "Do you want to come along?"

Brian stood tall and waved his arms. "Another case to solve. Right, Sammy? We'll call it the *Case of a Confused, Beat-up Man, Wandering Down a Back Road.*"

Sammy rolled his eyes. "Brian, I was wrong. You haven't changed a bit."

Chapter Three

The face, swollen and black-and-blue, showed little resemblance to Sammy's neighbor, Tom Boyer. His head was bandaged, and two painful eyes followed the boys and Mr. Wilson as they entered the room.

"Hi, Tom, it's Marc Wilson. Sammy's here with his friend, Brian. Can you talk?"

A weak voice said, "A little, but I'm hurting."

Brian winced. "Didn't they give you pills for the pain?"

"I guess, but I still hurt."

Sammy moved closer to the bed. "What happened to you?"

"After I got home from work, I took the dog for a walk. Two big guys got out of a car and attacked me. One of them had a bat. When I woke up, I was here in the hospital with a concussion and some bruises."

"What happened to your dog? Didn't he help you?" Mr. Wilson asked.

A smothered chuckle followed by a painful cough stumbled from Tom's mouth. Grimacing, Tom said, "That dog is a survivor. My wife told me he ran home."

"So why did these two men attack you?" Sammy asked.

Tom closed his eyes and kept them closed. Sammy thought at first that he had fallen asleep. Then Sammy realized it was Tom's way of escaping the question.

"Tom, I know it's painful, but maybe Brian and I can help you."

"Yeah, I can just see you and Brian with two thugs looming over you with a bat. I'll tell the nurse to prepare a bed next to me."

"Come on, Tom, you know what we do. We work with the police. Let us help you."

"I already gave this to the police. The guys beat me up. It was dark. I didn't see them clearly. That's it. I didn't know them, and I don't have any other answer."

Sammy stood quietly, staring at his neighbor. The super sleuth had used this interrogation technique before. When in a conversation, some people can't stand silence. They feel they must talk to fill the empty gap. If Tom Boyer was uncomfortable before, he was more so now.

Tom looked away to the large window and then up at the dark television set mounted on the wall. When that didn't provide the release he needed, he glanced back at Sammy. "They probably thought I was someone else. It happens."

Sammy remained quiet, motioning for Brian to do the same.

"Look, I can get into trouble. It's better this way."

"It must be some trouble if it's better to be in bed with a concussion," Mr. Wilson said.

"What did the men say to you?" Sammy asked, crossing his arms across his chest and waiting.

"Okay, okay, they said, 'If you or your boss, Harry Hoover, say anything, we'll be back.' Something like that."

"So you and Harry Hoover know something that could be harmful to someone. Is that right?"

"Yes, and I'm not saying anything more. It's personal."

Sammy nodded, showing no expression.

And waited.

"Relax, boys, I went to get advice from a lawyer two months ago. So I already have someone helping me."

"Who's your lawyer?" Brian asked.

"Michael Helm. Do you know him?"

Chapter Four

The amateur detectives couldn't wait. When they settled into the back seat of the car, they started to speculate.

"Two months ago, Mr. Boyer went to your father for help," Sammy said. "After that, the law firm transferred your father to California."

"Do you think that your neighbor had something to do with my father being sent away?"

"No, I'm not saying that," Sammy said, slipping his notepad from his pocket. "But I'm making notes. Mr. Boyer made two contradictory statements. One, it was dark. He didn't see them. Two, he didn't know them. If he didn't see them, how can he say he didn't know them?"

"I was thinking the same thing," Brian said.

Mr. Wilson smiled and kept his attention on the road.

"I imagine your father will have some interesting answers for us," Sammy said. "Will he be at your aunt's house this evening around 7 o'clock?"

"Yeah, but he can't reveal any information about a client. You know that. Right, Sammy?" When Sammy didn't react to his comment, Brian added, "That's privileged information. I'm lucky if my father talks at all when he comes home from work."

"I can understand why," Sammy said. "The law says a lawyer can't reveal information given to him by a client." He looked up to his right. "But Mr. Boyer mentioned something that could change that."

****

Aunt Catherine's house was a mile from the Bird-in-Hand Country Store. It was a brick, two-story structure with a large front porch. As Sammy turned his bike into the driveway, he saw Brian and Mr. Helm sitting on the porch. Sammy had been here several times before with Brian, always admiring the many flowerbeds and well-kept lawn.

Sammy rode his bike up to the porch and propped it against the railing. "Hello," he said as he climbed the steps.

Michael Helm was a small man. His lean face, thinning hair, and gray eyes belied the fact that he was a stern and stubborn individual. He stood and extended his hand as Sammy approached.

"I heard that we have a common friend, Tom Boyer," Mr. Helm said, shaking hands and then reclaiming his chair. "Technically, he's not my client anymore since I left the firm. I have my own office now."

The rocker squeaked as Sammy sat and put it into motion. "If I'm not getting too personal, why did you return to Lancaster?"

Mr. Helm frowned and shrugged. "I missed Lancaster and the people here. I know my wife and Brian did. They thought it was crazy to go to California to do the very things we were doing here."

Sammy pressed on. "Then why did you go?"

"When the managing partner of a law firm offers you a promotion and a pay raise to move, you don't say no. Lowe Construction is a big client of ours. Their biggest branch is in Oakland, California, so I was sent there."

The rocking stopped, and Sammy leaned forward. "But something happened that changed your mind. What was it?"

"I needed to come back. I . . . as I said, I missed the friends we left behind."

Sammy retrieved his notebook. "Brian told you what happened to Mr. Boyer, a neighbor of mine. He was punched around very badly. What trouble is he in?"

Mr. Helm took his time to answer. "I can't tell you even if he's a former client. That's privileged information. I'm bound not to reveal anything that he may have told me."

"Unless," Sammy said, "that information is already known by someone else."

Mr. Helm smiled. "You're assuming that other person is the party responsible for Tom Boyer's beating. And that information was the reason for the beating."

"No," Sammy said, "I'm suggesting that Mr. Harry Hoover, a co-worker and friend of Mr. Boyer, also knows the secret."

Mr. Helm sat back and crossed his right leg over the other. "Ah," he said, "you know the law, and you are quite right. If someone else has that information, then I am not obliged to keep the secret."

Sammy snapped his pen out of his pocket and readied his notepad. He wanted Brian's father to know he expected a lot of factual information.

Mr. Helm held his arms out in open fashion. "Since you are my son's best friend and mentor, I will tell all. Well, almost all. However, you both must promise me that you will not expose the information you are about to hear."

Sammy added, "Except to those who already know."

"Yes, I agree to that," Mr. Helm said. "I gave Tom Boyer my personal promise not to inform the authorities. I would feel bad if what I tell you somehow got to the police."

Sammy felt the itch that suggested Brian's father was trying to keep the problem from seeing daylight, which might indicate that he was somewhat involved. Sammy glanced at Brian, who shrugged and raised his eyebrows. Sammy then looked Mr. Helm in the eye and said, "Okay, we promise."

Mr. Helm took a deep breath then began. "Tom Boyer came to me with a secret. When his conscience faced that secret, he experienced guilt. That guilt brought him to our firm. When I saw Tom, he was in bad shape mentally. He had a lot of baggage to unload."

Brian leaned forward, his elbows on his knees and his head in his hands. "Dad, keep it simple. What was the secret?"

"Tom Boyer works for Lowe Construction. He was digging out one of the foundations for the new convention center. Tom was operating the track hoe, and his friend, Harry Hoover, was supervising. Well, this one time Harry yelled for Tom to stop the scooping arm. Harry saw something odd in the newly-loosened dirt." Mr. Helm hesitated. His face muscles tightened. "In the dirt were two bones."

Sammy paused from his note-taking. "Are you saying they uncovered an Indian burial ground?"

Brian's father continued. "By law, if any human bones are found during an excavation, the site is shut down to allow archeologists to come in and study the bones and any artifacts. This could close down the operation for months. According to Tom, Harry convinced him to forget about what they found, so no wages would be lost and the project would be finished on time. After a couple of days, Tom Boyer came to me to find out what trouble he could be in by keeping the secret. End of story."

"And what trouble is Mr. Boyer in because they didn't report it?" Sammy asked.

"Disturbing a human burial site and not reporting it constitutes a Class A misdemeanor. The men could be fined thousands of dollars and/or confinement in jail up to a year."

"What did you advise him to do?"

Mr. Helm lowered his head. "Nothing. He didn't ask for advice. He said he was going home to think about it."

"Did Mr. Boyer say what happened to the bones?"

"He told me Harry Hoover took them to his car. That's the last he saw them."

"And after your session with Mr. Boyer, you were sent to the West Coast," Sammy said.

"Yes, to handle the California-based Lowe Construction."

"Who sent you to California?"

"Walter Watts, the managing partner. He specializes in divorce cases."

"Did Walter Watts know about your client and the Indian bones?"

Mr. Helm nodded. "We have meetings where we discuss each of our clients. But all of it is privileged information. No one is allowed to discuss that knowledge outside the office."

Sammy looked to the street. That same white car had passed the house two times before. He resumed his attention back to Brian's father. "How soon after settling in California, did you decide to come back?"

"About two weeks."

Sammy pursed his lips. "That was after Brian was arrested."

Mr. Helm's head jerked. "What?"

"You decided to come back right after Brian was arrested and the charges were dropped."

Mr. Helm sat up. "Yes, I suppose so. Are you hinting at something here?"

"No, just getting my facts straight. And soon after your return to Lancaster, Tom Boyer was attacked."

"Well, if you're through, I'm going inside to relax. Trying to get organized again is tiring. I see it didn't take you boys long to return to the detective business. Good luck, and I hope you find out who assaulted Tom."

Sammy watched as Mr. Helm disappeared into the house. "Your father may have dipped his toe into the water."

Brian hunched his shoulders and closed his eyes. "There's another one of your metaphors. What does it mean?"

"Your father's a good man, Brian, but he might have made himself part of the problem."

"How do you know that?"

"Tom Boyer told your dad that his friend, Harry Hoover, also knew about the bones. It means your dad was aware that Tom's secret was not privileged information. Your father could have made that information public. He chose to ignore it and for good reason."

"Why?"

"Stan Lowe of Lowe Construction has money in the Lancaster County Convention Center Project. If the discovery of the bones becomes public, the project is shut down for a time, and Stan Lowe loses money—bundles of money. Lowe Construction is one of the law firm's clients. Your father must do what's best for Stan

Lowe. If your father exposes the discovery of the bones, his law firm loses a client and millions of dollars."

Brian's voice rose as he said, "Whatever my father did, he did for his clients. That makes him a good man. Right, Sammy?"

Sammy stood and went to the railing. He gazed up at the sky. "What about the dead Indians whose graves may have been destroyed?"

"That's it. The Indians put a curse on Tom Boyer and Harry Hoover for disturbing their graves."

"Why do you say that?" Sammy asked.

"Elementary, my dear Chief. Tom Boyer ended up in the hospital." Brian got up and straddled the porch railing. "I bet Harry Hoover is next."

"Really?"

"Oh, yeah, those Indian curses are like the Egyptian curses. You invade their tombs, and you are cursified."

"Cursified? I don't think that's a word."

"That's because you never experienced an Indian curse."

"And you have?" Sammy said with interest.

"Remember my cousin, Stevie Miller, who lives in Washington Boro? Nine years ago we were playing in his backyard. I was digging with a stick, and I dug up an Indian arrowhead. Stevie and I agreed to become blood brothers by cutting our hands with the arrowhead and mixing our blood."

"What happened?"

"Because I had used the sacred arrowhead, we were cursed. We became cursified. The cuts in our hands got real sore, like they were on fire. If I hadn't reburied the arrowhead back into the ground, who knows what would have happened?"

Sammy shrugged. "Who knows?"

"But because I replaced the arrowhead back where it belonged, the soreness was gone in one week."

"Amazing," Sammy said.

Brian's pressed lips made dimples form in his cheeks. "Are you making fun of me on our first day back together?"

Sammy glanced away from his friend. The white car was speeding away with the sun behind it. Sammy patted Brian's shoulder. "Be at my place tomorrow morning at 9 o'clock. We better check on Harry Hoover. Maybe he's been affected with the Indian cursification."

"Cursification? Is that a word, Sammy?"

"I hope not, Brian. I hope not."

Chapter Five

Mr. Wilson dropped the boys off at the convention center construction site on Vine Street. They soon spotted an opening that allowed trucks to enter and exit the area. It presented an invitation for them to enter the well-planned confusion. Following a worker carrying a wooden plank, the amateur detectives ventured into the forbidden area. They walked past two concrete trucks, waiting their turn to unload. Several multilevel structures gave height to the construction. Various cement block walls awaited closure to become rooms.

Brian pointed up. "Hey, look at that!"

A giant tower crane was lowering a tub of concrete to waiting workers below.

"Are you boys looking for something?" boomed a voice to their left.

The shock left Brian wishing he had stopped at a restroom before entering.

"We're looking for Harry Hoover. Is he here?" shouted Sammy over the din of a cement truck strewing its contents between wooden forms.

"Get over here," waved the man wearing a hard hat and a bad temper.

The boys followed him as he ventured 20 more feet away from the action. He unclipped his measuring tape and extruded 15 inches toward the intruders. "I'm Harry Hoover. What do you have for me?"

If the measuring tape had been a gun, it had the longest barrel Brian had ever seen. "We . . . we don't have anything for you. We—"

Sammy cut in, "I'm Sammy Wilson, and this is Brian Helm. We know your friend, Tom Boyer. He's a neighbor of mine. We visited him in the hospital yesterday."

"Yeah, so, what do you want?"

Sammy came right out with it. "We think he got hurt because of some bones that you two found here."

Brian stood tall behind Sammy. "Yeah, Indian bones," he said.

Harry glanced around, recoiled the measuring tape, and moved closer to the boys.

Brian took one step back.

"Did Tom tell you about the bones?"

"No, we heard it from someone else."

"It was that crazy dame from the sidewalk. Don't believe a word she says. We have our share of groupies. She was always waving at us. She has a thing for Tom."

"She likes Tom, does she?" Sammy said to keep Harry talking and believing the mystery woman could be their source of information.

"She was hysterical. One time she came running down here, saying she saw bones in a scoop of dirt. She said this used to be an Indian cemetery. She just wanted an excuse to get closer to Tom to talk to him. She's a lonely, crazy dame. She does and says anything to get attention. If I were you boys, I wouldn't believe anything she tells you."

"So there were no bones," Sammy said to make Harry Hoover's point clear.

"No, just pieces of rotten wood and stones."

Sammy motioned to the sidewalk. "Is the woman here now?"

Harry scanned the area. "I don't see . . . You said you talked to her. You should know if she's here or not."

"Thank you. We'll go look for her. Come on, Brian."

The boys walked out a different way, up the sloped driveway to King Street.

"What makes you think she's here on King Street watching?" Brian asked.

"Harry Hoover looked in this direction when I asked him if she was here. Also, he said she ran down to them. This block slopes down from King Street to Vine Street."

Brian bowed in mock reverence. "That's why you are the master, and I'm just your humble servant."

Sammy eyed his friend. "Will my humble servant start interviewing the spectators? See if they were witnesses to a woman who ran down the incline, shouting something about bones. You know how strangers socialize while engaged in a similar activity. Maybe someone talked to her."

"I'll start at the other end of the block," Brian said and ran ahead.

Sammy walked up another ramp that led to the parking garage that overlooked the construction site. A man had his camera pointed down as he leaned over the sidewall. The man glanced around as Sammy stopped near him. Judging from his camera gear, the man was a pro. Extra lenses protruded from expensive luggage.

"Are you taking pictures for the Lancaster Newspapers?" Sammy asked.

The man went back to working his camera. Sammy heard the whine of the zoom lens as the photographer composed the shot.

"I don't mean to ignore you," the man said, still looking through the camera onto the project below. "I've been waiting for two workers to be in position so the picture tells a story. I didn't want to miss the shot." He turned around and smiled. "I finally got it."

Sammy rested his arms on the low wall. "Are you here every day?"

"Almost. I saw you and your friend down there talking to a worker."

The aspiring detective grinned. "A zoom lens has a critical eye. Did you take our picture?"

The man again went back to his viewfinder. "Why were you in a dangerous area not wearing a hard hat?" he asked, concentrating on the scene below.

"We're looking for a woman," Sammy said and pointed. "Maybe you know her. Some time ago she ran down that ramp yelling about bones."

The camera clicked several times, and then swung around to Sammy and clicked again. When the camera lowered, the man smiled. "Oh, that lady. I was here the day she did that. She was talking to me, and suddenly she ran down to the men working the excavator. She had problems. You're not allowed to enter the work area. That's why they have a fence around most of it."

"Why did you say she had problems?" Sammy asked.

"Oh, did I? Well, she said she was divorced. She's man crazy. She had her eyes on the construction workers. To be honest, she's a bit nutty, a very negative person. She had nothing good to say about anything."

"What did she look like? Did she mention where she lived or worked?"

The man glanced up as though thinking, but his eyes followed the tower crane. Another tub of concrete was being delivered to the required destination. "Not where she lived, but I believe she is a nurse. She was about 5 feet 7 inches. Maybe thirty years old. Heavy set with dark, stringy-like hair. I felt sorry for her."

"Did she have her eyes on you?" Sammy asked.

"No, no, nothing like that. Her eyes were always on the two guys digging the dirt. She had a thing for the construction guys, I guess."

"Well, thanks for your time," Sammy said and went back down the parking garage ramp. Brian was at the bottom waiting for him.

"No luck," Brian said, raising his hands over his head. "How about you?"

"Brian, look over my shoulder. See the man with the camera equipment?"

"Sure, I see him."

"What's he doing?"

"Should I smile? He's taking our picture."

Chapter Six

Later that afternoon, after Mr. Wilson returned the boys to Bird-in-Hand, Brian threw himself back across Sammy's bed. His eyes roamed over familiar territory. The same cracks meandered over the bedroom ceiling. However, the jagged lines did little to hinder the clarity of Brian's thoughts that he projected there. The image was of a man wrapped in bandages in a hospital bed.

"Sammy, I was thinking. The only real damage done in this case is the attack on Tom Boyer."

Sammy rolled his chair out from behind the old oak desk to get a better view of his friend.

"You're forgetting another injustice," Sammy said. "Your father learned about the bones from Tom Boyer. If he exposed that information, Lowe Construction, his law firm's biggest client, would suffer a great financial loss. As a result, your family was sent to California, where you were arrested for stealing a purse. I'd call that damage also."

Brian visualized a skull and two crossbones.

"Yeah, and all because two bones were found in some dirt."

"I feel sorry for the Indians, too, if their burial grounds have been disturbed," Sammy said.

"Do you know what's wrong with this whole mess?" Brian said to the ceiling. "There's no evidence. No bones to prove that a . . . what did my father call it? A Class A something or other had occurred."

"A Class A misdemeanor," Sammy said and added, "with that to look forward to, I don't think Tom Boyer will be in a rush to confess his part in the cover-up. Even if he confessed, there are no bones to prove it. I can't imagine Harry Hoover giving up the bones." Sammy stood and went to the window. "And you're right, Brian. Without the bones, there's no case."

Brian sat up on the bed, his legs dangling over the side. "And who knows how many bones were carted away in the dump trucks? Although, it's been two months and nothing has turned up in the media about human bones being found."

"Do you think Harry Hoover threw the bones away?"

"According to Tom Boyer, Hoover took them to his car. I can't see anyone throwing something valuable away. They might still be in his car."

Brian jumped up. "Okay, let's go."

Sammy locked his hands behind his head and leaned back in his chair. "You go ahead, Brian. I'll catch up later."

Brian was halfway out the door when he turned and with a sheepish look said, "I don't know where I'm going, do I?"

Sammy smiled. "I was hoping you did. I was ready to follow you this time."

Brian's face lit up. "Oh, I know. Look in the phone book for Harry Hoover's address."

"Even if we find out where he lives," Sammy said, "we can't break into his car." Sammy frowned. "Do you want to be arrested again?"

Brian did a belly flop back on the bed and then rolled over. "My grandfather once told me, 'Brian, it's no fun growing old.'"

Sammy waited and then asked, "What's your point?"

"The point is, it's no fun getting arrested either."

"Right," Sammy said. "So we'll forget about stealing the bones from Harry Hoover and discuss something we're overlooking."

"What are we overlooking?" Brian said to the ceiling.

"Why were only two bones uncovered? If they are human bones, why wasn't a skull found? A human skull would certainly be with other bones of the body. A skull would be hard to overlook."

"So what are you saying?"

"I don't know what I'm saying. I'm just asking. Assuming the two bones found were human, where is the skull?"

"Yeah," Brian added, "and maybe the bones aren't Indian bones."

"That's a possibility," Sammy said with excitement in his voice.

"Wasn't there a house and some stores torn down to make room for the convention center? Maybe years ago someone was killed in the house or a store and buried in the cellar."

"And the missing skull?" Sammy asked.

"Oh, I know. They buried his head someplace else."

"Why would they do that?"

"So he couldn't be identified."

Sammy rolled his eyes. "Brian, if you looked at a skull, could you tell who the person was?"

The ceiling above Brian suddenly went blank. Images were not forthcoming from the amateur detective.

Sammy hated it when he made his friend feel small. He didn't want to belittle anyone, but he had no patience with people who couldn't think on his level. This was especially true with people he loved. Now, Sammy took the time to ease his guilt.

He sprang from his chair and went to the bed. He shook Brian's leg. "I must say your brilliant creative thinking has given me an idea for our next step."

Brian smiled.

"Peter Seibert is the director of the Heritage Center of Lancaster County's museums in downtown Lancaster. The museums are only a block away from the construction site. He must know the history of the area. I'm going downstairs to call him and make an appointment."

When Sammy left, Brian smiled at the ceiling and said, "See, I'm a brilliant creative thinker." He puffed out his chest and put his hands behind his head. "My outstanding creative thinking probably developed during my stay in California. Not everyone is a world traveler like I am. Sammy's smart, but he's never been out of Lancaster County. So, from now on, he'll have to depend on me for creative thinking."

Brian sat up, pushed himself from the bed, and stood by the open door. "Sammy," he yelled, "can I use my creative thinking on Peter Seibert?"

Chapter Seven

The Heritage Center of Lancaster County was in the first block of West King Street. It consisted of two museums: the Heritage Center Museum and the Lancaster Quilt & Textile Museum. Both were adjacent to the Lancaster Central Market.

"Are you sure this is right?" Brian asked, looking at the marble steps.

"Peter Seibert said these steps lead up to his office," Sammy said.

"But the Heritage Center Museum is several doors up the street."

Sammy flicked his hand. "Brian, just go up and open the door."

Brian went up the steps and turned the knob. "It's locked. Hey, there's a button and speaker here on the side."

"Well, push the button," Sammy said from the steps.

Brian pushed the button and waited.

A voice said, "Yes, who's there?"

"Who's there?" Brian asked.

"Who's there?" came the voice back.

"Who's there?" Brian asked again.

The voice repeated, "Who's there?"

Brian countered with, "Who's there? Say who's there when I say who's there."

Sammy pushed his friend aside. "I'm sorry. This is Sammy Wilson and Brian Helm."

A buzzer rang. "Come right up," said the voice.

"I wanted him to identify himself first," Brian said, following Sammy inside and up more steps. "It's a secret psychological technique I developed."

"How does it work?"

"Pretty good, actually. Thank you for asking."

Sammy rolled his eyes and shook his head.

The next door was unlocked.

Peter Seibert's office was cluttered with a mix of art, antiques, and modern office equipment. Sitting on a huge Victorian banker's desk were photographs of a woman and several children. Cubbyholes in the desk were filled with rocks, shells, and other items.

Mr. Seibert wore a well-worn tweed coat, a button-down L.L. Bean shirt, and chinos. His eyes matched his brown hair, graying at the temples. His mustache and six-foot height added to his directorship image.

Sammy was familiar with Peter Seibert's physical appearance. He had appeared in the media quite often with activities dealing with the Heritage Center's museums.

"Hi, I'm Sammy Wilson. This is Brian Helm."

They shook hands.

"Yes, I know who you are," Peter Seibert said. "You're . . . I was going to say amateur detectives from Bird-in-Hand. But you are hardly amateurs, more like professionals, I'd say."

Brian stood tall and, in his deepest voice, said, "Yes, tales of our crime-fighting exploits travel far and wide. I recently returned from California—"

Sammy interrupted Brian's monologue. "I'm sorry, we don't have time for that." Looking at Mr. Seibert, he asked, "Is there a place we can sit, so I can take notes?"

"Sure. Let's sit over there," he said, motioning to a table and chairs near the desk.

Sammy started the interview. "As I said on the phone, we're working on a case that might concern the convention center." Reading from his notebook, Sammy asked, "Do you know of any Indian burial grounds being located at the convention center construction site?"

With a grave expression, Peter said, "That's not something we like to talk about. This whole area is underlain with Indian burial grounds. The early settlers frequently built their settlements on sites of old Indian villages and adjoining cemeteries. After all, the land had already been cleared. Probably most of Lancaster is sitting on an Indian village, and the burials are all around us. The problem is that no one likes to talk about such things. The contractors and developers don't want to shut down their work because of finding remains."

Peter Seibert verified what Sammy had suspected. One more step remained, so Sammy asked, "Could there be any explanation for human, but not Indian, bones found at the convention site?"

"Absolutely," Mr. Seibert said. "There could be remains of settlers who lived in the area. Long before there were church burial grounds, people were buried close to their homes. It would be like a farm cemetery today. I'm sure there are plenty of private lots in this area."

Brian glanced at Sammy and said, "So anybody could have buried anybody, with or without a head."

Peter Seibert grimaced as he nodded. "Lancaster was a town way back. The burgesses would not have been too happy to have bodies everywhere. That leaves the possibility that bones found here today might have been buried years ago to cover up a killing. Murder is not new. It's possible that a body found today had been deliberately hidden a long time ago."

Sammy flipped a new page and continued to write.

Peter noticed and said, "It looks like you're writing a book."

"If we solve this case, I'll let Brian write the book."

Peter put his hand on Brian's shoulder and said, "I liked your 'who's there?' routine at the door. I saw that in an old horror movie. I like humor. It helps clear away the cobwebs of history."

"Really?" Brian said. "See there, Sammy, he likes humor, unlike some people I know."

The three stood. "Before I forget," Sammy said, "have you heard of any bones being uncovered at the convention center construction site?"

"Not so far," Peter said. "Why? Do you expect bones to be found?"

Sammy spoke before Brian had a chance. "With what you just told us, it seems logical. I thank you for the information. It gives us a lot to work with."

"I was glad to help," Peter said. "Just promise me one thing."

"What's that?" Sammy asked.

"Brian, when your book is made into a movie, promise me you'll get Brad Pitt to play my part."

Brian grinned. "I like humor in a historian."

Chapter Eight

The late morning sun pelted the young detectives as they descended the marble steps. Brian screwed up his face. "I need sunglasses."

"I can think of something better," Sammy said. "How about some ice cream?"

"Hey, yeah, that's cool, real cool," Brian said, producing an artificial smile. "Where do we go?"

"Let's go to the Creamery. My parents know the owners. It's right here, just around the corner on Market Street."

The boys rounded the corner, walked past the Central Market, and saw the Creamery placard. Tables with chairs gave customers an open-air eating experience.

Brian ran on ahead, then stopped and glanced back. "Why is the Creamery sign outside of the Lancaster Quilt and Textile Museum?"

"Because the Creamery shares the same building with the museum," Sammy said.

The teens followed the signs past the museum reception area to the Creamery.

The eatery was small, displaying the menu on several blackboards attached to the wall behind a long counter. Customers sat at tables along the opposite wall.

As the boys walked past a table, Brian's arm brushed against a glass bowl that held sugar packets. The bowl and its contents followed the law of gravity and landed on the tile floor. Broken glass and sugar packets marred the otherwise clean floor. Brian suddenly became the center of attention. All eyes were on the teenager.

Brian, being Brian, stood tall and said, "Now that I have your attention, I guess you're wondering why I called this meeting."

Everyone laughed, except Sammy. He rolled his eyes and advanced to the counter.

Several patrons collided as they bent down to help with the cleanup. The momentum sent one man back against a table, spilling coffee and a few choice words.

Jason Spatola, one of the owners, appeared with a dustpan and brush. After the broken glass and sugar packets were disposed of in a trashcan, a short, middle-aged woman skirted the counter. She presented a sales slip to the teenager. Brian glanced at the bill: $30. He looked up in disbelief.

"That bowl was cut glass," the woman said. "You turned it into broken glass."

Brian reached into his pocket, knowing his

funds were limited. He looked sheepishly at Sammy, who was stifling a laugh while holding two dishes of ice cream.

Sammy nodded toward the woman. "Brian, this is Beth Becker, part owner. I told her to write out the bill as a joke."

Everyone again laughed.

Sammy handed the dish of chocolate ice cream to his perplexed friend. "Come on, Brian. We'll eat these at an outside table."

Brian ran the plastic spoon inside around the dish to collect the soft ice cream. "I knew the bill was a joke all the time."

"You fooled me," Sammy said. "You looked really scared."

"I was perfecting my acting skills. You never know when they'll come in handy."

"How can I be sure your behavior is real or know when you're just acting?" Sammy asked.

"You never will. It's the price you pay for having a gifted and creative thinker as a partner."

Sammy realized the truth in Brian's statement. Much of Brian's behavior was based on his intuitive humor. On the surface, many of his remarks and actions seemed childish. But, in truth, they were creative ways of meeting his needs for attention and feelings of inadequacy.

Sammy finished his ice cream and reviewed his notes.

Brian pitched his empty dish and spoon into the trashcan. He wiped his hand over his mouth and chin and said, "According to Peter Seibert, the bones could be Indian or of an early settler."

Sammy glanced up. "However, that information doesn't do us much good. Like you said, Brian, 'Without the bones, there's no case.' We must find a way to recover the bones without stealing them."

"Oh, I know. We advertise in the newspaper for Indian bones and say high prices paid."

"It's illegal to own human bones unless you have a license to study them for research. No one, not even Harry Hoover, is going to announce that he has human bones for sale."

Brian frowned. "Oh, I know. We disguise our voice and phone Mr. Hoover on a cell phone. We say, 'People know you have the Indian bones. You'd better get rid of them.' Then we wait outside his house in your father's car, and when he comes out and drives away, we follow him. When he hides the bones in a woods somewhere, we get them."

"What if, instead of throwing them away, he grinds up the bones and throws them to the winds? What if he waits a day or two to dispose of them, or he keeps them?"

"Oh, I know—"

Sammy extended his hand in a stop position.

"Brian, let's take time to think."

"But, I was letting my subconscious creative thinking throw out ideas."

"If you took the time to think first, we wouldn't have to throw out your ideas. Your conscious thinking has roots in your subconscious." Sammy quickly lowered his head and went into his thinking mode as Brian muttered something to himself.

After several minutes, Sammy raised his head and opened his sparkling blue eyes.

Brian was watching, waiting. He knew the signs of a working plan. "You figured out a way to get the bones. Right, Sammy?"

"Yes, and it starts with enlisting the help of our friend, Joyce Myers."

CHAPTER NINE

Joyce Myers had aided Sammy and Brian on many cases. Her short brown hair, large hazel eyes, and oval face projected health and beauty for the fifteen year old. Her writing and photography skills were of immense help to the detective team. Many times her skills enabled her to go undercover into businesses, homes, and situations to collect evidence against individuals.

In *The Toy Factory*, she entered a factory to check out the building and interview workers concerning a smuggled computer chip. In *Amish Justice*, while researching information about Lancaster County farms, she protected a farmer who was experiencing a series of "accidents." In *Doom Buggy*, her camera captured suspicious activity while on a stakeout.

Now, Joyce was looking forward to the meeting with Harry Hoover, for it would test her power of persuasion as outlined in Sammy's plan.

"Yes, come in," Harry said upon meeting Joyce at the door. He turned to the woman who remained seated on the sofa. "This is my wife, Carol. Carol, this is Joyce Myers, the girl who's going to interview me for her school's newspaper."

Carol was a pretty, blue-eyed blond whose legs were curled under her. At first, Joyce thought that Mrs. Hoover had a physical disability that confined her to the sofa. Later, she discovered she was either lazy or had no social skills.

Carol nodded at Joyce and said, "I didn't know they had school during the summer."

"No, we don't. I just like to prepare ahead of time. In fact, I'm making ready two articles for the school paper to publish right after the start of school."

"What are the subjects?" Carol asked.

"Yours is one: the Construction Worker. The other one is called Modern Nurses in Training."

"You're not fooling me," Carol said. "I see what you're doing."

Oh, gee, Joyce thought, *has my masquerade been uncovered so soon?* "What do you mean?" she asked.

"The school is preparing the students for career choices: construction work and nursing. I'll bet you have other occupations selected for future articles."

"Yes, I have," Joyce said, much relieved.

Harry Hoover motioned toward a chair. "Joyce, sit over there, and I'll sit here next to my wife." He checked his watch. "I don't have much time. Let's get started."

"I don't have a lot of time either," Joyce said. "My father is waiting for me out in his car."

"Have him come in and join us," Carol said.

"He'd rather listen to his music in the car," Joyce said, lowering her camera to the carpeted floor and readying her notebook and pen. She read the first of her prepared questions. "When I think of construction activity, I think of hard work that is dangerous and physically demanding. Is that true?"

Harry placed his hands behind his head and flexed his muscles. "You may not know this, but construction work is the most dangerous work done on land. We have to be in good shape. All day long we are standing, bending, stooping, lifting and carrying heavy objects. Plus, we're exposed to all kinds of weather."

"What you just said might turn the students away from selecting such a job."

"Yeah, it is work, dangerous work, but it's a challenge to go to your job every day. You know that you are contributing to the creation of something important. Like now, part of my life is in the Lancaster County Convention Center. That structure and the adjoining Marriott Hotel will stand for centuries."

"You said construction work is very dangerous. What makes it hazardous?"

"I believe the most dangerous safety hazards are falls from heights, being crushed by vehicles, and being hit with falling objects. Wait just a minute," Harry said and hurried to the adjoining room. He returned wearing a hard hat and an orange-colored jacket. He pointed upward. "For safety reasons, we wear hard hats." He looked down. "I have on steel-toed boots.

And this bright-colored jacket makes me very visible to the other workers."

"This is great," Joyce said and grabbed her camera. "Stand right there, and I'll get some shots to illustrate the article." Joyce maneuvered around to compose the best shot. "You make a wonderful model."

Carol Hoover shifted position on the sofa and said, "Yes, I think I have a very handsome husband."

The zoom lens focused on Harry's head. "I want to get a close-up of your face and the hard hat. These additional close-up shots add reality to the article. Right now, I'm trying to find some bones to photograph to enhance my article about nurses. One nurse told me they must study bones, because bones can tell you about the past health of individuals, about sicknesses they had and have today."

Without moving, Carol said, "Harry, you have some bones in the family room. Let her photograph them."

Harry's body quivered. "Well, ah, sure, okay. But they will have to stay here in the house."

Harry disappeared into the next room.

Joyce said to Carol, "That's fine. If you have a paper grocery bag, I can lay the bones on it. That way, they will have a plain background."

Carol Hoover struggled off the sofa. "I have some bags out in the garage. I'll be right back."

Joyce slipped into the next room and listened. From the direction of the sounds, Harry was in the basement. The teenager then went back into the living room and waited.

"Here's the bag," Carol said when she returned. "Where do you want it?"

"Put it on the floor. I'll shoot down on them. Where did your husband get the bones?" Joyce asked.

"They're deer bones. A friend of his gave him the bones. I don't understand why he wants to keep them."

Harry entered the room, holding two bones. "They're deer bones, not human. Is that okay?"

"They look human to me," Joyce said. "They'll be fine."

Mr. Hoover glanced down. "Do you want them on the paper?"

"Yeah, great," Joyce said and stood above the brown paper and waited while Harry centered the bones on the brown background. One bone was long, the other one shorter.

When Mr. Hoover moved away, the camera zoomed in and out, capturing many shots. Joyce knelt down, rearranged the bones, and continued snapping away.

When Joyce stood, she thanked Mr. Hoover for use of the bones. Not wanting to put excessive attention on the bones, she quickly turned the conversation back to construction workers. "How do you get along with your fellow workers? Do you consider yourself as part of a team?"

"That's exactly right. We are a team. For instance, Tom Boyer is a co-worker and great friend. He operates the track hoe that scoops out the dirt. Sam Thompson takes the dirt to a landfill in his dump truck. Marty Miller and others bring in the concrete to structure the foundation and walls. Many of our workers are of Spanish descent. I've learned a lot of Spanish from them. It comes in handy."

"Yes," Joyce said. "It's easier to get a job these days if you're bilingual."

Harry moved toward the door. "You should have enough for your article. If you need more, give me a call."

Joyce shouldered her camera, clutched her notebook, and smiled. "Thank you for the interview. I know you will be hearing from me."

When the door closed, Harry glanced at his wife and then down at the bones. Had he made a mistake?

Chapter Ten

It was 8:30 in the evening, but Sammy and Brian had agreed to wait for Joyce until 9:00. If the planned charade took longer, they had arranged to meet at 9:00 the next morning.

Brian was stationed at the window, Sammy at his desk. The computer was on and ready to go. Sammy checked his watch. They still had half an hour.

"What are the chances that he still has the bones?" Brian asked. "And, if he does, what are the chances he'll let Joyce photograph them?"

Sammy patted the arms of his chair. "We have a better chance because Joyce went than if she hadn't gone at all."

"We play the odds. Right, Sammy?" Brian said and then bent closer to the window. "Oh, oh, it might be them. I believe her father's car just pulled in."

Sammy and Brian faced the door, waiting, hoping it was good news.

Joyce was hugging her camera and breathing heavily as she rushed into the bedroom. "You were right, Sammy. He fell for it. I have pictures of the bones right here."

Sammy smiled and shimmied his chair closer to his desk and the monitor. He glanced up at Joyce. "Did you have any trouble?"

"None at all," she said, resting her camera on the desk. She extracted the memory card and handed it to Sammy.

Brian could hardly contain himself. He watched as Sammy leaned over and slid the card into its proper computer slot. He stood on one foot, then the other. "These computers are so slow," he said and glanced at Joyce. "How many bones did he have? How big were they? Did he tell you where he got them?"

Joyce nodded toward the monitor. "You'll see them here in a minute. There are two bones. One large, a leg bone, I think. The other one was smaller, maybe an arm bone."

With a couple of clicks, the computer downloaded the complete file of photos from the memory card. Sammy located Joyce's photos in the My Pictures folder. "There must be twenty to thirty pictures here," Sammy said. "Oh, good. The last ones are of the bones." He double-clicked on the first thumbnail bone image. A large, screen-size picture appeared, showing great detail.

"So there they are, the mysterious bones," Sammy said. "Did Harry say why he had them?"

Joyce folded her arms across her chest. "He told his wife they were deer bones. He had them downstairs in the family room."

"Now what do we do?" Brian asked.

Sammy retrieved the memory card from the slot, gave it to Joyce, then reclined back in the chair. "We can prove Harry Hoover has two bones. We have a female eyewitness who saw Tom Boyer and Harry Hoover dig up bones at the construction site. We know Tom Boyer went to consult with a lawyer, Brian's father, about finding the bones. Tom later was brutally attacked by two men. My first thought is to turn this information over to Detective Ben Phillips. However, we can't. We promised your father not to tell anyone about the bones. My second thought is to visit Walter Watts. He is the law partner responsible for transferring your father to California. Was it to protect their client, Lowe Construction, or was there another reason for the transfer?"

Brian raised a finger. "I'll bet Walter Watts was the one who beat up your neighbor, Tom Boyer."

"Only three other people knew that Tom Boyer might talk about the bones that were discovered: your father, Walter Watts, and Harry Hoover. I know your father didn't do it. Tom is Harry's best friend. That leaves Walter Watts."

Brian raised his hands to his head. "But if we go to see him, he'll know that we know. He might have us beat up, too. I'm allergic to baseball bats. They give me lumps and bruises."

"But we'll have the advantage," Sammy said. "If two men approach us with a bat, we'll know they're not from our local baseball team, the Barnstormers."

Chapter Eleven

The driver watched the girl and her father pull away from the parking space and head west on Main Street. The man in the back seat was more concerned about the boy who was mounting his bike.

The white car pulled in next to the boy.

"Hey, ain't you Brian Helm, the famous boy detective?" the driver asked.

It was late, and Brian needed to get home, but a fan was a fan. He smiled and stood tall by his bike.

The man stuck a pen and paper out the car window. "Could I have your autograph?"

Brian quickly dropped his bike and reached for the pen and paper. When he did, the second man snuck up from behind and forced a damp cloth to his face. In seconds, Brian's limp body was in the car, lying next to a baseball bat.

The white vehicle sped away as Sammy watched helplessly from his bedroom window.

****

Brian's eyes opened with great difficulty. Or were they open? No, he was dreaming, for before him was a North American Indian, sitting in front of a fire. The Indian threw white powder into the flames. A bright flash and billowing smoke rose up and out through an opening in the wigwam.
Wigwam?
Where am I? What's going on? Brian wondered. He shook his head to regain some kind of reality, but the dream-like action streamed before his eyes.

The Indian stood and danced around him, chanting unfamiliar sounds while beating a drum and shaking rattles down over his body. Feathers and beads flipped and flopped about as the Indian's head bobbed up and down. Animal skins covered the body. Dabs of paint obscured the face.

The dancing continued for many minutes, then stopped. The Indian knelt beside Brian's head and said in broken English, "My ancestors' bones disturbed. You now possessed with curse."

Brian raised his head and saw that he was lying on bark mulch inside an Indian wigwam. "What do you want?" he asked.

"I am medicine man. My magic drive out evil spirits that cause sickness. You much sick with evil spirits. You give bones to me. My ancestors cannot rest. Their spirits not free until bones returned to me."

"But I don't have the bones," Brian said.

The Indian's eyes bored into Brian. "You know where bones are. Get them or I not remove curse from you," the Indian said and held a damp cloth over Brian's face.

Chapter Twelve

Sammy, his mother, Brian's parents, and Detective Ben Phillips had gathered outside the Bird-in-Hand Country Store. The detective was in constant contact with patrol cars searching for a white vehicle containing two men. Sammy's father was in the house checking the hospitals.

The limited street lighting plus the speed of the abduction had offered Sammy little in the way of clues. The position of the white car as it pulled in and out kept the license plate hidden. Hooded sweatshirts prevented a reliable description of the two kidnappers.

Mr. Helm took Sammy aside. "I feel responsible for this whole thing. They are using my son to threaten me."

"But why?" Sammy asked.

"To keep me quiet about the bones. What else?"

"Were you warned before?"

"I received a phone call in California after the purse-snatching episode with Brian. The voice demanded I not say anything about the bones, ever.

He said they had control over my family, using Brian's arrest as an example. That was the first warning. Now, I fear this is the second warning."

Sammy agreed. "They don't appreciate your return to Lancaster County, thinking you are going to spill the beans."

"Yes, and I haven't decided what to do."

"Hey, everybody, listen up," Detective Phillips yelled, standing outside his car. "They found Brian. He's okay."

Mrs. Helm and Mrs. Wilson hugged and cried tears of joy. Then Mrs. Wilson ran into the house to tell her husband that Brian was found and was okay.

"Where is he?" Mr. Helm asked.

The detective, sporting a large frame, receding hairline, thin mustache, and penetrating eyes, lifted his chin and said, "Back on Gibbons Road. They're bringing him here in a patrol car. What's going on here, Sammy?" Detective Phillips asked.

Sammy saw Mr. Helm shake his head. He remembered his promise not to mention the bones. "I'm not sure. Let's wait and ask Brian."

"How about you, Mr. Helm, anything to say?"

"Not at this time. Maybe later."

Detective Phillips scratched his head and frowned. "First, it was Tom Boyer and two men, and now it's your son and two men. Both Tom and Brian were found back on Gibbons Road. That seems to be a common dropoff point for whomever is behind whatever is going on." Detective Phillips fixed his eyes on Brian's father. "How many more people have to be rescued from Gibbons Road before I'm told the reason?"

The question went unanswered as a patrol car rounded Beechwood Road and stopped in front of the store.

Brian popped out, unassisted, and produced his mechanical smile. His mother and father rushed to hug him and to confirm that he was all right.

When everybody was satisfied that Brian had survived the kidnapping ordeal unharmed, Sammy said, "Brian, your pants are wet."

"Don't ask," Brian said

"What happened?"

"I've been cursed."

"What does that mean?" Sammy asked.

"I've been invaded by evil spirits, and they won't leave until their bones are returned to the Indian."

Sammy glanced at the detective then back at Brian. "What Indian?" he asked.

"The Indian witchdoctor," Brian said.

With outstretched hands, Detective Phillips said, "Let's take this inside, so I can get Brian's statement. People are starting to gather. Is that all right with you, Mr. and Mrs. Wilson?"

"Yes, let's go into the kitchen," Mrs. Wilson said.

It was nearly 11 o'clock that night when they sat around the kitchen table. Only Mr. Helm sat back against the wall. Sammy assumed that Brian's lawyer father would soon have a decision to make. He would have to reveal the bones' discovery at the construction site.

The detective readied his notepad on the table. "Okay, Brian, tell me what happened?"

"I was getting on my bike to go home, and a white car drove up. This was right after Joyce and her father left. The driver recognized me and asked for my autograph. He had a pen and paper, so I went over. I didn't see the other man leave the car. All at once, he came up behind me and stuck a rag to my face. Then I blacked out."

"Possibly chloroform," Detective Phillips said.

"Next thing I knew, I was lying on bark in a large wigwam."

The detective stopped writing. "How did you know it was a wigwam?"

"The tent-like structure and the Indian sitting in front of a fire was the first clue," Brian said and smiled.

"I'm sorry," the detective said. "I shouldn't interrupt you. Go ahead, continue."

"It was like a dream. This Indian threw something into the fire. A bright light flashed and smoke rose up and went out an opening at the top. The Indian danced around me, beating a drum that hung from his neck. He chanted those weird Indian sounds and paraded strings of beads and feathers up and down my body. It was scary. He said I was cursed until the Indian bones were given to him. Then I woke up on the road back there."

Mr. Helm caught his son's eye. He frowned and shook his head.

"Ah, that was some dream, wasn't it?" Brian said, downplaying the incident. "It must have been the chloroform. It had me hallucinating."

Detective Phillips pressed on. "What did the Indian mean about returning the bones?"

"I don't know. I asked the Indian that. 'What bones?' I said . . . in my dream, of course."

"So it was all a dream," the detective said. "I suppose the two men who snatched you were in your dream, too."

"No, no, they were real."

"They put you to sleep so you could have this dream, and then they dumped you back on Gibbons Road?"

Brian checked his father, who gave a slight nod.

"Yep, strange, isn't it?"

"Can you describe the two men?"

Brian thought a while. "No, it was dark, and they wore these hooded sweatshirts."

"And the rest was just a dream," the detective said, nodding his head with his eyes closed.

"It had to be a dream, because at the end, the Indian rose up and disappeared up through the hole in the wigwam," Brian said, adding a touch of drama.

Detective Phillips closed his notepad and stood. "Just like I'm going to disappear through the kitchen door. I'm going home to bed. When someone is ready to tell me what's going on here, see me at the station. Please inform me before *Number Three* turns up on Gibbons Road."

Sammy felt sorry for Detective Phillips as he left the house, but a promise was a promise. If the detective knew about the bones being found at the construction site, he would have to report it. By law, any human bones dug up must be reported to the authorities. The police then contact the medical examiner to examine the bones. He then determines whether a crime has been committed.

At midnight, alone in his bedroom, Sammy sat at his computer. *Someone had disguised himself as an Indian to scare Brian*, he thought. *Apparently, the object was to scare us into getting the bones from Harry Hoover. That doesn't make sense. The harm done to Tom Boyer was to prevent him from revealing the find. So was sending Brian's father to California. First it was "keep quiet about the bones," and now it's "make them known." Are we dealing with two different villains?* Sammy wondered. *No, it had to be the same person, because the criminal acts had a common denominator: the same two thugs.*

Sammy pulled up Joyce's photos of the bones. Here was the proof that the bones existed. Were they Indian bones or other human bones? Was there a difference?

He clicked on one close-up of the two bones and zoomed in until the image filled the screen. He saw where the larger bone could fit into a socket. Pores were evident on the bones. A long, thin, faded streak marked one bone. *What caused that?* Sammy wondered.

The teenager zoomed in on the streak. He clicked the filter button, then selected sharpen. The blur focused. A recognizable pattern formed. Or was it just Sammy's imagination? Maybe it was the late hour. He was tired. He rubbed his eyes, shook his head, and looked again in disbelief. He wondered, *Why would a human body, buried for decades, produce bones displaying numbers and letters?*

Chapter Thirteen

Looking at the monitor the next morning, Brian agreed. He saw what could be a 3 and a 6. Of course, he also saw a one-eared rabbit and a distorted fork. Brian's imagination was primed to accept the unreal. The weight of the Indian's curse had stolen hours of sleep the night before. Even Sammy's insistence that curses were only illusory, dramatic deceptions, left Brian unchanged.

Sammy made several printouts of the smudge. With a pen, he outlined what he considered to be a faded 3, a 6, and an L and an A. He gave one print to Brian and asked, "How did the writing get on the bone, and what does it mean?"

Brian squinted and voiced a couple hums. "Maybe Harry Hoover put it there and then tried to wipe it off."

"What reason would he have? If he kept the bones, and we know that he did, why deface them? If he was going to sell the bones to a collector, why devalue them with writing?"

"Oh, I know. Mr. Hoover has been in the construction business for years. Maybe he's collected bones for a long time. This bone could be Number Thirty-six in his collection."

"Then why do the numbers and letters look faded, like they were rubbed off?"

Brian shrugged. "Maybe it's a strip of bacteria forming letter-like and number-like shapes. Did you check the other bone for marks?"

Sammy nodded. "Apparently, the large bone was the only bone Joyce turned over while taking the different shots." He considered another explanation. "Just being in the ground over decades could fade and wear away any man-made markings."

Brian backed up to sit on the bed. He missed by several inches and slid to the floor. With his back against the bed, he glanced up into Sammy's eyes and said, "You should have a wider bed."

Sammy displayed a rare grin and added, "Either that or less floor space."

Brian glanced around the room. "Everyone should sit on the floor more often," he said. "It gives you a new perspective. It humbles a person."

"You can use a little humbleness," Sammy said.

"What do you mean? I'm in great shape. I have an outstanding personality. I probably have more humbleness than anyone."

"I rest my case," Sammy said.

Remaining on the floor, Brian went back to studying the printout in his hand. "Putting marked bones into the ground wouldn't be a crime, would it?"

Sammy went from his desk to the rocker. "I imagine it depends on where and how you got the bones. But the question now is: If it is writing, was it put on the bone before or after it left the ground? The only way to prove it is to ask Mr. Hoover."

"But he won't admit to having the bones."

Sammy pushed with his feet, putting the rocker into motion. "We can show him the pictures Joyce took."

"That should do it," Brian said. "Let's go."

"We can't now. He's at work. We'll go to his house tonight."

"When he sees Joyce's pictures of the bones, maybe he'll go to the police," Brian said, anxious to rid himself of the evil spirits put on him by the Indian witchdoctor.

"Brian, do you think your father will release us from our promise not to tell the police about the bones?"

"My dad doesn't talk much. When he does, I listen. My mom will give me a warning when I goof or misbehave. If I hear from my dad, I know I'm in real trouble."

"Are you saying your father will only speak up if someone's in real trouble?"

"He said he promised his client, Tom Boyer, that the authorities would not be told about the bones. That is, unless he or his friend, Harry Hoover, went to the police. My dad is sticking to that promise." Brian stood from the floor and raised his index finger. "However, if things got out of hand, my father would do the right thing."

"You don't think your father is protecting Lowe Construction?"

Brian shrugged and put his hands into his pockets. "What do I know? I'm only a kid with a curse hanging over him," he said.

"Brian, there is no curse, no real Indian. It was only an act to scare us into returning the bones."

Brian swept his hand over the seat of his pants. "Well, something pulled this bed back when I went to sit on it. Let's face it, Sammy. I'm jinxed."

"Think about it, Brian. These are not your average Indian bones dug up at a construction site. They may not be Indian bones at all. The marks on the bone may prove that. Therefore, there's no curse involved."

"Then why the Indian? And why does he want the bones if they're not Indian bones?"

"That, Brian, is what we have to investigate."

Mrs. Wilson's voice snaked up the stairway. "Sammy, phone!"

"Okay, I'm coming," Sammy said, jumping up from the rocker.

"You need a cell phone," Brian said, as Sammy passed the bed. "Everybody in California has one."

"Cell phones could be dangerous to your health and your wallet," Sammy said, hurrying down the steps.

Brian lay back on the bed and consulted the ceiling. "Isn't that right? We need cell phones. If

Sammy and I had cell phones, I could have called him from the wigwam last night. I'd hand the phone to the witchdoctor and have him talk to Sammy. While he was talking, I'd jump on him from behind and tie him up. Then I'd yank away the feathers and wipe the war paint off his face and see if he's a real Indian. Then I'd call the police . . . if only I had a cell phone."

The ceiling made no comment.

Sammy returned. "That was Detective Phillips. He's sending us a guest."

Brian rolled on his side and glanced up at Sammy. "Who?"

"He didn't say, and I didn't ask him." Sammy went to the window and peered out. "Detective Phillips is mad at us right now, and I don't blame him."

Brian sat up on the bed. "I'll bet our guest has something to do with the bones."

"At this point, I'll take any bones he can throw at us."

"Wow, was that a bit of humor from the Samuel Wilson?"

Sammy lifted his chin. "Yes, and I make no bones about it."

"Gee, what's putting you in good spirits?"

"I'm not really. It's a cover-up for what Detective Phillips said about the guest he's sending over."

"What did he say?"

"She's Number Three."

Chapter Fourteen

The woman Sammy's mother escorted into his bedroom was plain and in her thirties. She was neither a beauty nor unpleasant to look at. Her shoulder-length black hair had tight curls. Her brown eyes, slightly blunt nose, and thin lips were offset with a ruddy complexion. She wore an embroidered blouse and jeans.

"Do you want me to stay?" Mrs. Wilson asked the woman.

"No, that's all right," the woman said.

When Mrs. Wilson left the room, Sammy introduced Brian and himself. He offered the rocking chair to their visitor.

"So you ended up on Gibbons Road."

"Yes, just like Brian."

"Tell me about it."

"First of all, my name's Grace Landis. I'm a nurse at the Lancaster General Hospital. This morning, I got out of my car in the parking lot, and a man forced me into a car with another man. They put something over my face, and I passed out. I woke up in a teepee with an Indian dancing around me."

The boys glanced at each other.

"He told me to tell the police that I saw bones dug up at the convention center site in Lancaster. When he finished harassing me, he covered my face with a cloth. I passed out again and woke up on Gibbons Road."

"How do you know bones were found at the construction site in Lancaster?"

"I was there. I was watching when the big machine dug them up."

What luck, thought Sammy. "Are you the woman who ran down into the site, claiming you saw bones?"

"You bet I am. And those two workers made fun of me, saying they saw no Indian bones. But they did, and they took them and hid them."

"What made you think they were Indian bones?"

"Everyone knows that Indian villages were here before Lancaster became a settlement. And Indian villages mean Indian graveyards."

"I'm curious," Sammy said. "Why didn't you report the discovery to the authorities?"

Grace rolled her eyes. "Yeah, right. What chance would a divorced crazy woman with no proof have against two lying men?"

We have the proof now, Sammy thought, *but we can't tell you about it because of a promise we made. If we told you, you would go to the police.*

"So what are you going to do?" Sammy asked.

"I thought you could tell me," Grace said sharply. "Isn't that why the police sent me to you? You're supposed to be the big-shot, young detectives investigating the Indian bones."

"Did you tell Detective Phillips about your encounter with the Indian and about the bones?"

"Yes."

Sammy wasn't pleased. There would come a time when Detective Phillips would have to act on the information. "What did he say?" Sammy asked.

"He said that I was to come here and report to you."

"Did he mention Brian's experience last night?"

"No, he didn't mention Brian at all." She glanced at Brian sitting on the bed. "Did the Indian threaten you, too? Do you know where the bones are?"

Brian looked at Sammy, who said, "We can't comment on an ongoing investigation."

She sat up abruptly, highly annoyed. "Then you must know where the bones are."

"Sorry, we can't comment," was all Sammy could say.

Sammy and Brian were still. They felt helpless.

Grace Landis flew up with such force that the rocker slammed back against the windowsill. "Tell me where they are. I'll put them back. They're going to hurt me if I don't get the bones," she said. She hurled herself at the desk and grabbed at the bones' photos.

Sammy pulled them away and stepped back from the desk. "Sorry, but I downloaded these bones from the computer." Which was not a lie.

Brian snapped up from the bed and waved his arms around. "Tell her, Sammy. Tell her there's no such thing as a curse. Tell her that the Indian and his two thugs won't beat her up. Tell her we are as frustrated as she is. Tell her that our hands are tied. Tell her what our day is like, day in and day out. Tell her—"

Grace Landis lunged at the open door, yelling, "You guys are crazier than they think I am. You males are all alike. Thanks for nothing." Her voice faded as she descended the stairway.

Both boys were left gaping at the doorway.

When Sammy recovered, he asked, "What was the hand waving and 'tell her this and tell her that' all about?"

"That was dramatic acting. Good, huh? I wanted to confuse her. Get her mind off the bones, get her to settle down so we wouldn't have to lie to her."

Sammy raised his eyebrows and patted Brian on the back. "I must admit it worked."

Brian sniffed a couple of times and tugged at his pants. He stood tall and said, "Maybe I should have stayed in California. Hollywood wants guys like me."

"Based on your acting ability?"

"Not just because of my great acting skills, but because I got arrested. Hollywood goes for stuff like that. After you're arrested, you have to say you're sorry though. Then they make a movie of your life."

Sammy stood stiff, clapped a hand on his friend's shoulder, and said dramatically, "Lancaster County needs you here, Brian."

Brian swept his fingers back over his hair and walked away from under Sammy's hand. "That's true. I must fight the evildoers," he said, swiping back the window curtains and looking down onto Main Street. "Those are my people down there. I must protect them. And I am ready to defend them with my life." He turned and showed his mechanical grin.

Sammy shook his head. "I'm glad you got that out of your system. Now, do you feel better?"

Brian slumped and shuffled back to the bed. "Not really."

"What's the problem?"

"My father."

"What about him?"

"He won't allow us to tell Detective Phillips about the bones. And that makes me wonder."

"Wonder what?"

"Who will be Victim Number Four?"

Chapter Fifteen

"I'm sorry your dad had to leave our law firm," Walter Watts said, as he guided the boys to chairs around the conference table. The lawyer wore a dark hairpiece, quite noticeable for its lack of gray. His bushy salt-and-pepper eyebrows overhung his brown eyes. An expensive business suit slouched over his bulky frame.

Brian slid a tied bundle of law books across the table. "Here are the books that belong to you. My father took them by mistake when he packed his stuff."

"I got the impression when you called that you wanted more than just to return my books. When you said your friend, Sammy Wilson, would join you, I thought I might be in trouble. The media coverage of your crime-fighting exploits is impressive."

Brian said nothing in return, because Sammy pinched his thigh.

"Look, your dad is a good lawyer. That's why I sent him out west. There was nothing sinister in my decision. It was best for him and best for the firm."

Sammy ventured into deep water. "It seems strange that Brian's father was transferred soon after conferring with a client, Tom Boyer."

Walter Watts sat back in his chair, his round face flushed. His breathing increased as he stumbled over words. "What—eh—how—how do you know Tom Boyer? Mr. Helm should not have talked to you about him."

"He's a neighbor of ours. He works for Lowe Construction Company. And, by the way, we know about the bones." Sammy let that sit and soak in for a while, and then added, "We know Stan Lowe is a client of yours. He stands to lose money if his construction site closes down."

Now it was Brian's turn to stir the pot. "Yeah, and yesterday afternoon, we checked around and found that you also invested in bonds offered by the Lancaster County Convention Center."

When Walter's head hit the back of his chair, his hair started a ripple effect that advanced his hairpiece one inch beyond his normal hairline. Its quick repositioning demonstrated years of experience that no manual instructions could ever achieve.

Walter Watts' portly figure eliminated him as the Indian or either of the two thugs. One option remained, so Sammy took a chance. "We know about the Indian and the heavy hitters whom you hired."

The lawyer's eyes showed whiter. "What's that mean? What Indian? What heavy hitters?"

"One man has been sent to California," Sammy said. "One man was beaten. Both were warned not to tell about the bones. Two other people have been kidnapped and entertained by a dancing Indian. Both were instructed to recover the bones. Mr. Watts, will you explain what's going on here?"

"No, but I can add to the confusion."

"How?"

"I'm being blackmailed."

Chapter Sixteen

The boys looked at each other.
Walter Watts closed the door to the conference room and pulled folded papers from his coat pocket. He checked them and laid one on the table. "This is the first letter I received."

Sammy read the message aloud. "Human bones were found buried at the Lancaster County Convention Center site. They were not reported. Unless you pay me $50,000, I will tell the police of these bones. More later."

The lawyer returned to his chair. "I got a phone call one day later. A man's voice asked me if I had the money ready. I told him I would not be blackmailed. He hung up without a word. About a month later, I received this letter."

Sammy read the second paper tossed on the table. "This is your last warning. Unless you pay $50,000, I will tell the police that you know about the bones dug up at the downtown construction site."

Mr. Watts tapped the table. "A day later, he

called. I told him again I would not pay him any money. He got mad and hung up."

"Why did you refuse to pay?" Brian asked.

"Unless somebody else heard about it, only Tom Boyer and his co-worker, Harry Hoover, knew about the bones. I figured it was one of them who sent the blackmail letter. What could they do if I didn't pay up? If they told about the bones, they would only get themselves into trouble."

"And so you refused to pay," Sammy said.

Walter nodded. "I'm telling you this in confidence. I assume you boys will say nothing on this matter."

"We promised someone we would not talk about the discovery of the bones except to those who already know. We are keeping that promise."

"In that case, I will tell you another interesting fact."

"What's that?" Sammy asked.

"Stan Lowe is also being blackmailed."

Chapter Seventeen

"This case is like the Energizer Bunny; it just keeps going and going and going," Brian said.

"Stan Lowe came to me for advice," Walter Watts said. "He showed me his blackmail letter. It was identical to mine. I told him I received one like it, and I refused to pay. I told him why." The lawyer shrugged. "I haven't heard from him since. So whether he paid or not, I can't tell you."

"I'll bet everyone who has money invested in the project is being blackmailed," Brian said.

Sammy pushed his hair away from his eyes. "You may be right, Brian. And if that's true, how many have paid the blackmailer?"

Walter Watts nodded and then grinned. "Whoever it is doesn't seem to be well organized with definite goals. If I hear from him again, maybe we can set a trap for him."

"You mean set up a payoff package and grab him when he picks it up?" Brian asked.

"Something like that," Walter said, standing with great effort and leaning forward on the table. "What do you say? Isn't that what amateur detectives do to catch their man?"

"Can you put together $50,000 to pay the blackmailer, in case something goes wrong?" Sammy asked.

"What can go wrong?"

"The blackmailer might ask you to show him the money. He may suspect a trick."

"Okay, but I'd hate to lose $50,000."

"I'm sure you'll get your money back and nab a blackmailer at the same time," Sammy said. "However, I'll only agree to do it if Brian and I plan and execute the operation."

"I'll agree, but no police are to be involved."

Sammy extended his hand, and they shook on it.

Walter Watts smiled and pushed the tied bundle of books across the table. "Here, Brian, take your father's books back. They aren't mine."

Chapter Eighteen

Sammy was tempted to call Stan Lowe, but what could he say? "I hear you're being blackmailed?" The contractor would insist that Sammy explain his source of information. The amateur detective could not do that or reveal any knowledge of the bones.

Instead, Sammy considered the only sensible option open. He and Brian would confront Harry Hoover with the bone photos. As a result, Harry Hoover might choose to dispose of the bones. But if he did, the photos remained as evidence, especially with Joyce's testimony. This action would force Mr. Hoover to confess. Sammy was counting on Harry Hoover to do the right thing and inform the authorities himself. Either way, the case would be over, and the fat lady could sing, while the Energizer Bunny rested.

****

The ranch house was part brick and part vinyl siding. The hodgepodge of bushes and flowers gave the lawn a presentable appearance. The Sentra parked in the driveway gave hope that Harry Hoover was home from work.

Smoketown, like Bird-in-Hand, was a peaceful village. It had a barbershop, restaurant, grain mill, gift shops, a veterinarian, and even a small airport. Peaceful, yes, but people still locked their doors at night.

Sammy glanced around as Brian and he laid their bikes over on the lawn. He found it strange that Mr. Hoover's front door was wide open with no screen-door protection from flying insects.

"The front door's open," Brian said. "He saw us coming. Right, Sammy?"

Sammy reached around to his back pocket and retrieved the photos. "I don't see Mr. Hoover. Do you?"

Brian ran ahead. "He's inside waiting for us."

"Stop, Brian. You may be right, but—'Come into my house, said the spider to the fly.'"

Brian stopped and backed up. "He wouldn't hurt us, would he?"

Sammy waved Brian back further. "This may be nothing, but let's play it safe. I'm going inside. If I don't appear and wave at you in a few minutes, go for help."

Sammy stepped up to the open doorway and looked in. The living room was empty. He stepped inside. "Hello, anyone here? Mr. Hoover?"

He continued into the next room. "Anyone—"

A figure bolted from the kitchen in a flying leap. The force sent Sammy backpedaling until he was flat on his back in the living room. The photos from Sammy's hand ended up on the carpet.

Sammy rolled several times and waited for another attack. None came. Instead, the figure of Harry Hoover loomed over him. The heavy breathing and wild look told Sammy not to move.

Harry picked up the bone photos. "So you sent the girl. Clever. And you came here to steal the bones. Where are they?"

"Don't you hurt him," Brian yelled in from the open doorway. "I called the police."

"Why would you call the police? You broke into my house. Now, where are the bones?" Hoover asked, bending down and yanking Sammy up from the floor.

"The bones are supposed to be down in your family room," Sammy said.

"I just came from there. They're gone."

Sammy held out his empty hands. "We don't have the bones. Brian and I came to see you about them. Your front door was open, so I walked in."

Since the boys made no attempt to escape, Harry sat in his recliner. With eyes closed, he said, "The door was open when I arrived home. I went through the house, thinking I could surprise the intruder. The kitchen door window is broken. That's how he got in. Then I saw you. The bones are gone. Somebody took them."

"Is your wife here?"

"No, she's at her sister's place, taking care of the baby."

Sammy pointed to the photos held by Mr. Hoover. "What are you going to do about the bones?"

"What bones?"

"The bones you took from the construction site," Brian said.

Harry glanced around the room. "What bones? I don't see any bones."

"Okay, Mr. Hoover, play that game, but we have pictures and Joyce Myers as a witness."

"You mean Joyce took pictures of some bones I showed her. Big deal. How are you going to prove the bones came from downtown Lancaster?"

"A woman, Grace Landis, saw the bones in the dirt."

"Ha, what she saw from one hundred feet away were pieces of wood. That's all."

"Brian and I know what you're doing, but think about it. You can't blackmail the investors if you no longer have the bones."

Harry Hoover sprang up out of the recliner and pointed to the door. "I'm not blackmailing anyone. Get out of my house!"

"One last question," Sammy said. "Did you write on the bones?"

"No, I didn't." Harry held the photos for Sammy to see. "Look at your pictures. Do you see any writing?"

"As a matter of fact, I do," Sammy said. He paused and, after a moment of insight, added, "I also see the handwriting on the wall."

Chapter Nineteen

"Somebody's been messing with my rocking chair," Joyce Myers said, as she stood and rearranged the cushions.

Brian glanced away from the ceiling and pointed at Sammy, sitting behind the desk. "I won't name names, but I know who sat in it last."

Joyce wiggled as she backed into the cushions, forming her own comfort zone. "Ah, that's better," she said and activated the rocker. After five floorboard creaks, she said, "Okay, what's next in your investigation? How can I help?"

"Someone has stolen the bones from Harry Hoover, and he will not confess to taking the bones from the construction site."

"But I saw the bones. I photographed them," Joyce said.

"As Harry Hoover reminded us, we can't prove those bones came from the construction site. We put ourselves in a bind when we promised Brian's father not to reveal information about the bones. Unless Mr.

Helm changes his mind or someone else goes to the authorities, our hands are tied."

"Your seeing 'writing on the wall' was one of your metaphors. Right, Sammy?"

"Mr. Hoover said something that got me thinking in another direction. I need to think it through before we investigate further."

"Phone call, Sammy," Mr. Wilson yelled from downstairs.

Brian raised his head. "Uh-oh. What now?"

"I'm coming," Sammy said, heading for the steps, taking two at a time.

"What was California like?" Joyce asked, making conversation until Sammy returned. "You weren't there long."

Brian made a face at the ceiling. "They live a faster life out there."

"I thought you liked plenty of action."

"It's horrible out there. Half of anything that doesn't move they cover with graffiti. The other half they smoke. I think that's why you see a lot of Californians on skates."

"Brian, you're crazy."

"See? And I was only in California two months."

"I missed you," Joyce said. "Sammy really took it hard when you left. But if you tell him what I just said, I'll deny it."

"Sometimes I wonder how other people in the world feel, not having met me. It must be sad for them, going through life Brian Helmless."

"Brian, stop right there, before I take you off my 'People I Tolerate' list and put you on my 'People I Don't Want To Know' list."

Before Brian could answer, Sammy slipped into the room and settled at his desk. "Well, it happened," he said. "The bones were stolen yesterday, and today Walter Watts got a phone call. 'Pay $50,000 or I take the bones to the police.'"

Brian sat up on the edge of the bed. "What did the lawyer say to the blackmailer?"

"Mr. Watts acted scared and told the man that he was ready to pay."

"Good, he wants us to jump into action. Right, Sammy?"

"The caller told Mr. Watts to put the money into a shoebox wrapped in brown paper. He's to go to Musser Park in Lancaster tomorrow noon and wait for instructions by way of the cell phone."

"Musser Park is on the corner of Lime and Chestnut Streets," Joyce said.

Sammy nodded. "Yes, and only several blocks from the construction site and Mr. Watts' law firm."

"So what's our plan of action?" Brian asked, rubbing his hands together. He was anxious to bring down the bad guys. "We'll hide in the bushes, and, when Mr. Watts hands over the money, we jump the blackmailer. Right, Chief?"

Joyce sat up and leaned forward in the rocker. "Okay, Mr. Watts waits in the park. But what if the phone call tells him to go somewhere else that requires a car?"

"I thought about that," Sammy said. "The blackmailer told Mr. Watts to *go* to the park. He didn't say to *drive* to the park. So, unless he's told to take a cab, I believe the exchange will happen right there in the park."

"I was thinking, we hide in the bushes and—"

"No, Brian, we don't hide in the bushes."

"We could hide behind some benches."

"No, Brian, we hide out in the open."

"Yeah, right," Brian said. "We wear a sign that says, 'Hey, we're hiding from you. Pretend you don't see us.'"

Sammy rolled his eyes and raised his arms. "What do you expect to see in a park?"

"Grass, trees, and kids playing."

"The blackmailer will be looking for undercover cops pretending to be maintenance men or something like that. He won't expect teenagers."

"So if he sees kids playing, it's natural."

"Now do you get it, Brian?" Joyce asked.

"Sure, we hide behind some kids playing."

"Brian!" both Joyce and Sammy yelled.

"Okay, I'm kidding. That was going to be my second suggestion. We throw a ball around or something. When the exchange goes down, we rush in and grab the blackmailer."

"Hold on," Sammy said. "It may not be that easy. The blackmailer is an amateur, but he's not dumb. We have to plan for the unexpected."

"I saw this in a movie," Joyce said. "A man stood holding a briefcase full of money. A man and woman on a motorcycle rode by and grabbed the money."

"Yes, I saw the same movie," Sammy said. "There has to be two people: one to drive, and one to take the money."

"But that didn't happen in a park," Brian said.

Joyce shook her head. "No, it was along a road."

"I doubt that will happen," Brian said. "They don't allow vehicles in a park, especially one as small as Musser Park."

Sammy went to the window and stretched his arms. "What else could happen?"

"There's another scenario that's quick and simple," Joyce said.

Sammy clapped. "Okay, let's have it."

"The blackmailer assumes that Mr. Watts will walk from his office to the park. What's to prevent the blackmailer from snapping up the money soon after Mr. Watts leaves his office?"

Sammy stood by the rocker. "That's good, Joyce. We can prepare for that with Brian and I, as two kids, casually walking behind Mr. Watts. We follow him to the park. If something happens we jump in; if not, we continue to the park and pretend to play when we get there."

Joyce offered another scenario. "Suppose the blackmailer has a child pick up the money. You grab the child, and he says a man told him to get the package."

"So we follow the boy," Brian said

"The boy is going to be watched," Joyce said. "If you're seen following him, you're in trouble."

After a moment of silence, Brian said, "Here's another scenario. Mr. Watts refuses to pay the blackmail, so the guy goes to the police with the bones. Presto, we find out who is behind this mess."

"The blackmailer won't go to the police. He's proved that twice before with Mr. Watts. He has never carried out his threat to report the bones. The best way to find out who is behind *this* mess is to catch him in the blackmail plot."

Sammy glanced down at Joyce, wondering whether to include her in their scheme. Her camera could capture valuable evidence, but the outcome was unpredictable. An element of danger existed. He decided to let it up to Joyce.

"Joyce, do you want to go with us to the park tomorrow? You'll fit right in—a teenager with a camera. There could be some danger."

"You can't have an adventure without some danger lurking about. I'm ready for an adventure. It will be exciting, photographing nature while a blackmailer is operating nearby."

"I was hoping, if Brian and I fail, that you might get a picture of our mystery man."

"I'll try my best."

"Great! I'll call Mr. Watts at 9 o'clock in the morning. I'll go over what we talked about here. I think it best to tell him he's not to get into any cars if instructed to do so. If we can keep the money exchange in the park, we'll have more control over the situation."

The Indian Bones' Revenge   103

"Do you know what's going to make this work, Sammy?" Brian asked. "The blackmailer won't be expecting teenagers to take him down."

"Let's meet here at 10 o'clock tomorrow morning. We'll go over each of our courses of action. My father will then drop us off near the park."

Brian shifted his weight on the bed. "Can your father stick around, in case there's trouble? Remember Detective Phillips won't be there to back us up like he usually does."

"Brian, Mr. Watts and your father said no police. We are honoring their wishes. However, if you see a gentleman reading a book while sitting on a bench, he might resemble my father."

"Oh, I can't wait," Joyce said.

"Have your camera ready for action," Sammy said. "Tomorrow at noon in Musser Park, the *red* rose, the *yellow* buttercup, and the *black*mailer will be in full bloom."

Chapter Twenty

The man reading on the bench also watched the pretty teenage girl at the park entrance. Her camera zoomed in and out as she moved from red rose to red rose. She stood back and recorded the sign to H. M. Musser Park, and then she entered.

The car parked across the street at William's Apothecary had arrived thirty minutes earlier. The figure inside wore a ball cap, dark glasses, and a mustache. He held a coffee cup to his lips and winced at the cold flavor change. He hung the paper cup out the window, releasing it to the gutter below.

A loud knock from inside the drugstore window caused the man to look. He followed a rigid finger down to the abandoned coffee cup. He opened the car door, recovered the cup, and slammed the door shut. He mouthed the word "sorry" at the unhappy face. The last thing he needed was to make a scene.

When the face disappeared from the window, he picked up the binoculars and watched the woman walking her dog in the park. He panned to the man reading a book, and then to the man asleep on the next bench. He stopped at the girl with the camera, paused, and then laid the binoculars aside. A drop of cold coffee slithered down his chin as he pressed the cell phone to his face. "Nothing yet," he reported.

Two teenage boys wearing sweat suits argued over who was going to dribble the basketball. A short robust man in a brown suit, walking ahead of them, seemed preoccupied. He hugged a brown paper-covered shoebox as he trudged up Chestnut Street.

As they neared the park entrance, Sammy bounced the ball to Brian and whispered, "It looks good so far."

Reaching for the bounced ball, Brian yelled, "Hey, get the ball to me the next time."

"You don't know how to catch a ball. That's the trouble," Sammy yelled as they entered the park.

"Yeah, well, catch this one before it hits the ground." Brian bounced the ball toward the man reading on the bench.

Sammy ran and caught the ball near the man's head. "Do you see anything yet, Dad?" he whispered.

Mr. Wilson, holding the book up to protect his face from the bouncing ball, said, "Nothing yet, but be careful."

Walter Watts decided to stop several yards beyond the man snoozing on the bench. He wasn't informed exactly where in the park to wait for the phone call. At the far end was a playground area for young children. He hoped the payoff didn't occur there. He felt strange, holding the small box filled with $50,000.

The boys whizzed past him, trying to outdo each other, bouncing and catching the basketball.

Then it happened.

His cell phone rang.

The lawyer balanced the box in one hand and slipped the phone from his pocket. "Hello," he said.

"I'm only going to say this once so listen. You're about 15 feet away from a man sleeping on a bench. Do you see him?"

Walter Watts turned his head. "Yes, I see him."

"Wake him up and give him the box. You then walk away, out the park, the way you came in."

Mr. Watts waited for more instructions, but the conversation was over. He closed the phone and put it away. He glanced around, looking for signs of the blackmailer. He had to be close by to know he was standing 15 feet from the sleeping man. He saw no one suspicious.

Joyce sat down on the wrought iron bench at a table. She relaxed her arms and took a deep breath.

"Hey, girl, take our picture," Brian yelled, holding the ball above his head and tossing it to Sammy.

Joyce rose slowly with the camera. "Okay, hold the ball and smile." She positioned herself so Mr. Watts was in the background. She zoomed in and focused on his brown package and waited for what came next.

The trio had agreed on this plan of action. When the lawyer put his cell phone away, that was the signal for the boys' photo session to begin. Joyce's camera from that moment on was to stay with the package and the person holding it. She was to photograph what happened.

Joyce stood closer to the boys, but she had her camera focused on Mr. Watts and the package. "He's moving to the man sleeping on the bench."

Sammy pinched Brian's shoulder as they stopped smiling at the camera. "Brian, don't you dare turn around," he said.

Brian snatched the basketball from Sammy. "Take another picture, one with me holding the ball," Brian yelled.

Joyce pretended to snap another shot. "He's shaking the homeless man," Joyce said.

"How do you know he's homeless?" Brian asked.

Sammy grabbed the ball from Brian. "Give me the ball," he said angrily. He added softly, "He's probably homeless because he has a torn knapsack under the bench with his belongings spilling out."

"The man's sitting up now," Joyce said. "Uh-oh, Mr. Watts handed him the package."

"A homeless man is our blackmailer?" Brian asked, wanting so much to turn around and see the transaction. "Let's go jump on him."

"What's he doing with the box?" Sammy asked.

"The homeless man is sticking it under the bench with the rest of his stuff."

"What's Mr. Watts doing?"

"He's walking away, back out the way we came in."

"What's the homeless man doing now?"

"He's just sitting there."

Sammy passed the ball to Brian and said loudly, "Go sit down at the table. You're a troublemaker."

"Hey, you come, too, or I'm going home," Brian replied.

The trio sat on the bench that faced the homeless man.

Sammy used his peripheral vision to observe the man, while pretending to be interested in Joyce's camera. "Strange, he's not moving. Is the package still under the bench?"

Joyce inspected the zoomed image. "Yes, it's with his other stuff."

"I don't understand why he doesn't get up and go. He's making no attempt to get away." Sammy elbowed Joyce. "Keep taking pictures of the man and the package," he said.

Joyce clicked off more shots, and then checked the memory card. It could hold 114 more pictures.

Sammy shrugged at his father sitting on the next bench, as if to say, *we don't know what's happening either.*

Seemingly, out of nowhere, a figure hustled across the grass. There was no doubt as to the man's destination. The homeless man reached under the bench and had the brown package ready. The individual grabbed the shoebox, turned, and bolted for the sidewalk. In that moment of unexpected intrusion, everyone sat frozen in disbelief.

"Oh, no, you don't," Brian said, as he stood and threw the basketball as hard as he could at the man.

The ball struck the man in the back. The package fell to the ground.

The man hesitated momentarily, left the package on the ground, ran, and hopped down onto the sidewalk.

Mr. Wilson got to the fallen package first, followed by Sammy and Joyce. Brian ran straight for the sidewalk. When he got there, he saw the man get into a white car across the street and drive away. Brian turned around, walked back, and glanced at the package on the ground. "Does this mean that we have to do it all over again?" he asked.

Sammy stooped and recovered the shoebox. His facial muscles tightened. "The only bright side is that he didn't get the money."

"Be careful," Joyce said. "You can still get fingerprints off the paper."

Sammy shook his head. "No, we can't. I noticed he was wearing latex surgical gloves, which I thought strange."

"Why would he do that?" Mr. Wilson asked. "He expected to take the money with him."

"That's what I don't understand," Sammy said.

Walter Watts joined the group after reentering the park. "Well, it didn't work. Now what?" he bellowed.

"I have no idea," Sammy said, handing the package to the lawyer. "You at least get your money back."

Mr. Watts took the package and examined it for damage. "This isn't the same package," he said. "This isn't mine. I used clear tape to seal the paper. This tape is reinforced with string."

Suddenly it came to Sammy why the man wore surgical gloves. He knew he was going to leave the package behind as a decoy.

They all turned around.

The bench was empty.

The homeless man, the knapsack, and the money were gone.

CHAPTER TWENTY-ONE

The monitor's brightness helped to dispel the gloom that filled the bedroom.

"Dumb, dumb, dumb. I should have anticipated our opponent's genius. Using the knapsack to switch packages was clever," Sammy said, as he slid the memory card into the computer.

Brian stood tall. "I thought I was kind of clever with the basketball. What I did was, I estimated the distance, the wind's velocity, his running speed—"

"Yeah, yeah," Joyce interrupted. "Brian, admit it. You closed your eyes and threw the basketball as hard as you could. It was a lucky shot."

While concentrating on the screen, Sammy said, "I hate to burst your bubble, Brian, but Mr. Blackmailer would have found another excuse to drop the fake package, like pretending to trip or something. Their plan was to switch the brown packages and leave the fake package behind to distract us, while Mr. Homeless Man escaped with the real package of money."

"I thought that Mr. Watts would have put cut newspaper in the shoebox instead of real money."

"How do we know he didn't?" Sammy asked.

"Hey, that's right," Brian said.

"If he did, the blackmailer is going to be mad. Real mad," Joyce said.

"Okay, I have Joyce's pictures downloaded and ready to go. See if we can salvage anything from our fumbling attempt to stop the blackmailer."

The trio examined the photos one by one but discovered no clues. However, they concluded both Mr. Homeless Man and Mr. Blackmailer had worn disguises. Because of their size and actions, they could be the same men who had attacked Tom Boyer and abducted Brian and Grace Landis.

Sammy brought up the close-up thumbnail of the bones. He zoomed in and the dark smear covered the screen. "Joyce, what do you make of the smudge there?"

"A crack in the bone might have caused it," Joyce said and pointed. "Hey, that looks like a three, and is that a six?"

Sammy waited.

"Oh, my," Joyce said, "I can't believe it, an L and an A." She looked at Sammy. "Somebody wrote on the bone."

Sammy sat back. "But who, when, and why?"

Joyce glanced at Sammy. "Did the other bone have the same writing?"

"From what I can see, you only photographed the one side of the smaller bone. We don't know what's on the reverse side."

"Maybe Mr. Hoover wrote on it."

"I thought the same thing. Maybe he catalogued his collection of bones that were dug up at construction sites."

"He told us he didn't write on any bones," Brian said, walking to the bulletin board.

Joyce raised a bobbing finger. "I know one place in Lancaster that catalogues bones. That's the North Museum of Natural History and Science."

"That's our next area of investigation," Sammy said and swung his arm out to Joyce. "Do you want to come with Brian and me?"

"You don't need me," she said and stooped to extract her memory card from the computer. "I'll take my camera and go home. Let me know what happens later."

Joyce turned back at the opened doorway and asked, "Why would someone bury marked bones?"

"Joyce, the answer to your question may be the pivotal point to this case."

Chapter Twenty-two

The Museum of Natural History and Science was close to downtown Lancaster. It faced College Avenue and was close to Franklin and Marshall College. The Museum displayed many collections and featured hands-on exhibits.

Mrs. Wilson parked the car in the side parking lot and was as anxious as the boys were to explore the potential treasures inside the building. The doors that led to the gift shop opened promptly at 10 o'clock. Sammy's mother paid the entrance fee and left the boys to their amateur sleuthing.

"Hello," Sammy said to the female greeter. "We would like to talk to the person who knows about bones."

"Alison Mallin is the person you want. Do you have an appointment?"

"No, sorry."

"And your names are?"

"Sammy Wilson and Brian Helm."

"Well, let me see if she's free," the greeter said

and dialed a number. "Alison? Sammy Wilson and Brian Helm are here to see you about bones. Are you free? Okay." She replaced the receiver and motioned toward the steps. "Her office is upstairs. She'll meet you in the hall."

"Thank you," Sammy said and watched Brian fast walk to the steps.

The woman who met them was 5 feet 3 inches with dark brown hair and brown eyes. She was middle-aged with a medium build. She was dressed casually in khaki pants and a white blouse. Her smile was as welcoming as the opened door to her office.

Sammy offered his hand. "Hello, I'm Sammy Wilson, and this is Brian Helm."

After Brian shook her hand, he asked, "Where is the restroom?"

"Down the hall," she said. "You'll see the sign."

It wouldn't mean anything, but Sammy felt obliged to issue a warning anyhow. "Brian, please don't make any side trips. Come right back."

Brian raised his arms as he walked away.

Sammy tried to relate to the theme of Alison's office, but he was overwhelmed by its immense offerings. The office was crammed full of fossils and insects. DNA and other models added to the scientific atmosphere of the room. Books and publications were plentiful on the two worktables and desks.

When Sammy's attention returned to business, he said, "Brian and I are investigating a case that involves two uncovered bones."

Alison Mallin sat behind her desk and motioned

toward a chair for Sammy. She took a deep breath, and then asked, "First of all, are you talking about human bones?"

Sammy opened a folder he carried that held the photos of the bones. First he produced an overall shot of the two bones. "Here is one photo," he said and laid it on her desk.

"Yes, they are human bones," Alison said without hesitation.

Sammy then handed her the glossy photo paper print of the extreme close-up that had been sharpened and enhanced for detail. "What do you make of the marking on the one bone?"

Alison Mallin studied the photo, frowned, and glanced at Sammy. "The identification number on the bone is worn away, but this is one of the museum's Indian bones."

Sammy couldn't believe it. How could buried bones, recently unearthed, belong to the North Museum? "How do you know they belong to the museum?"

"See the 3 and the 6? Archeological site numbers are written on each bone. Number Thirty-six is a code number for Pennsylvania. The LA is Lancaster. The other catalogue numbers are missing. Where are these bones?" she asked.

"We don't know. All we have now are the photos. How long have the bones been missing?"

Alison sat back and crossed her legs. "We have over 10,000 Indian bones in our collection. We did do an inventory several months ago. A couple of bones were unaccounted for. These apparently are two of them. We weren't too concerned about the loss, because we sometimes loan out bones to researchers. But now that you say these are floating around out there somewhere, they must have been stolen from the museum."

"Can you tell us who might be in a position to steal bones from here?"

"The bones are locked up in a room downstairs. It could be a staff member, a volunteer, or any one of the cleaning crew."

"Could you get me a list of names of these people so we can compare them to the people who are associated with this case? You need only go back a year."

"I can show you the list now," Alison said. She slid over to her computer and clicked an icon. "Come around the desk and have a look."

Sammy scanned the list. He paused at one name and pointed. "Do you know this person?" he asked.

"No," she said. "We have many volunteers. I don't know them all. Sorry."

The name Sammy saw, not only confirmed his suspicions, it helped connect some dots.

Alison was looking at the two photos that lay on the desk. "If someone stole the bones, and you don't know where they are, how did you get photographs of them?" she asked.

"You have been very helpful and kind, but I can't give out details of this ongoing case. Later, if things go right, we hope to return the bones to you." Sammy hesitated, and then asked, "Does the North Museum have any connection to the building of the Lancaster County Convention Center?"

"Not that I know of. Why?"

"Can you tell me why anyone would bury these marked Indian bones at the construction site?" Sammy put the photos back into his folder.

"No, but take away the writing on the bones, and I'd say someone wanted to stop the construction."

Brian had not returned

"Thank you for the help, and as I said, when we find the bones, we will turn them over to the museum. If Brian comes back, tell him I'm in the gift shop."

"I hope your friend is all right," Alison said.

"Yeah, I'm okay," Brian said, standing by the open door. "I was talking to a group of school kids up the hall."

Sammy shook his head. "Did you make them believe you were a great scientist?"

"No, I was honest. I told them I was a great detective."

Sammy smiled, went for the door, and turned back to Alison. "When Brian is off the leash, he's unpredictable. Other than that, he's a great friend."

Chapter Twenty-three

When Brian, Sammy, and his mother arrived home, the super sleuth was ready to make some phone calls. But that was put on hold when his father called Brian and him into the store.

"This man wants to talk to you, Sammy. He's Stan Lowe. He's doing the construction work for the Lancaster County Convention Center."

Sammy knew who Stan Lowe was. He was one name on his list to call. In fact, Sammy now recognized this man as the central player in the Indian bones' game.

What did Stan Lowe want? Sammy wondered. *It has to be about the bones.*

Stan Lowe, who was inspecting bolts of quilt material, turned abruptly. He was tall, thin, and dressed casually in a clean shirt and jeans. His tanned, stern face, stamped with wrinkles, commanded attention.

"I've been talking to your father. Now I need your cooperation," Stan Lowe said. "My lawyer tells me you amateur detectives are stirring up trouble about some bones uncovered at my construction site."

Brian's Adam's apple moved up and down as he maneuvered behind Sammy.

"I'm here to tell you to stop interfering in my business. My health is barely hanging on. I just got over a nasty divorce. I'm losing my hair. We're running overtime at the job. We're already two months late. Expenses are increasing. The hot weather slows down the workers, and accidents are on the increase. Sammy, your father tells me you boys are trying to help. If you want to help me, stop what you are doing."

"Mr. Lowe, we know that someone is blackmailing you. Your lawyer, Walter Watts, has already paid money."

"Yes, he told me that you botched an attempt to catch the blackmailer."

"We underestimated the opponent, but we learn from our mistakes. We know you've been threatened with blackmail. Have you paid them yet?"

Mr. Lowe glanced around. All the customers were in the rear of the shop inspecting the Amish quilts. "No, I have not paid, and it's none of your business," he said.

Sammy moved closer and lowered his voice. "Please, I need to know if you intend to pay. I have information that may change your mind."

"I am overwhelmed with personal problems, plus the details and responsibilities of my business. This matter with the blackmailer is like swatting a fly off my face. I'm willing to pay to make it go away.

The last thing I need now is for Indian bones to stop construction. "

"We believe there are two thugs and an Indian involved."

"A real Indian?"

"Maybe, or someone disguised as an Indian."

"There are millions of dollars tied up in this project. Two hundred thousand dollars is little compared to the profit involved."

Sammy was ready to explain that the Indian bones were planted at the construction site recently. The bones really belonged to the North Museum, and he need not pay off the blackmailer.

Suddenly, a surge of understanding helped Sammy create a better idea.

"Mr. Lowe, how would you like to pay off the blackmailer, get the bones, and reveal who is blackmailing you at the same time?"

"How is that going to happen?"

"The next time you get a call, you tell the blackmailer that you don't want to cause any trouble. You don't want the police involved. Tell him you want to make this a business deal, not blackmail. Tell him you will buy the bones for $200,000, no questions asked. However, to be sure the bones you are buying are the bones uncovered at the construction site, Tom Boyer and Harry Hoover must identify them. You'll only pay the money if you receive the bones that were unearthed at the construction site."

"And he'll agree to that?"

"Yes, if you promise not to prosecute him for any

actions he has taken against you. To guarantee him no harm, the meeting is to take place in your lawyer's office."

Stan shook his head. "I can't believe the blackmailer will agree to those terms."

"He will if you make one more demand."

"Which is?"

"Tell him you'll only deal with the Indian."

Chapter Twenty-four

The North Duke Street law office was alive with activity. The blackmailer had called Stan Lowe the previous day and, after settling minor details, had agreed to the terms. All individuals involved with the Indian bones were contacted and consented to be present in the law office.

Sammy had spent the last two days confirming what he already suspected. He then arranged for Alison Mallin and Grace Landis to arrive at 6:30 that evening. He ushered them into Walter Watts' empty office until they were needed. The others were to arrive at 7 o'clock and meet in the conference room.

Walter Watts sat at the head of the table. Tom Boyer and Harry Hoover sat to his left. Stan Lowe sat at the end of the table. Next to him was an empty chair reserved for the Indian. Sammy and Brian sat in the next two chairs. Two extra chairs were available against the wall, should the two thugs appear.

Sammy made a final scan around the table. Walter Watts sat forward, pleased and confident that his client,

Stan Lowe, would soon have the bone issue resolved. Tom and Harry appeared anxious. Sammy thought Stan Lowe would thank them, if he hadn't already, for keeping quiet about the bones. The briefcase in front of the contractor showed his willingness to settle the problem he thought existed. The aspiring detective wondered what Mr. Lowe would do when he found out the truth. The Indian bones had come originally from the North Museum and not Indian burial grounds in his project.

The empty chair caused Sammy to rethink his theory regarding the solution to the case. The name he saw on the North Museum's volunteer list was the keystone that held the other clues together. His conclusion pointed to only one person.

Brian Helm had gone into his secret agent, Double-oh-Seven and a Half, mode. He sat tall and probably thought he was a giant among men, but Sammy saw his knees shaking.

Sammy leaned forward and said, "We're all here except for the Indian. While we're waiting, Mr. Watts, will you go over the terms of the agreement?"

"Simply put, Stan Lowe has agreed to buy the unearthed bones for $200,000. In order to verify the bones are the originals, Tom Boyer and Harry Hoover are here to identify them. There is no blackmail involved here. It's strictly a purchase. The authorities or police are not to be involved in any way in this business transaction."

The conference room door opened further. Someone listening had entered the room. Everyone's head turned.

The Indian Bones' Revenge 129

The Indian immediately was in contrast to the others at the conference table. Feathers, headband, beads, war paint, and skin clothing made their way to the empty chair. A plain carryall bag was upturned on the table. Two bones rattled out in front of Stan Lowe. The Indian remained standing and looked briefly at those present. A fixed stare focused on the contractor of the Lancaster County Convention Center. "There bones. Now money," the Indian grunted.

Stan Lowe pushed the bones down the table to hard hats, Harry Hoover and Tom Boyer. "Are those the bones you dug up?"

Harry leaned over, his eyes inches from the bones. He nodded. "Yep, these are the ones." Tom agreed with Harry.

Stan Lowe unsnapped the briefcase and shook bundles of money onto the table. "Okay, I'll buy them for $200,000," he said.

"Ugg," the Indian said and nodded. A buckskin-covered arm guided the money into the carryall bag held at the table's edge. When the last packet was in the bag, the Indian looked at Walter Watts. "This money mine to keep, no strings attached. That right, Mr. Lawyer?" the Indian grunted.

Mr. Watts opened and outspread his hands. "Yes, that's right."

"How about money I got from you? No strings?"

Walter Watts stood and faced the Indian. His features grew tense. His mouth opened to speak when a cough from Stan Lowe stopped him. The lawyer glanced at his client and saw the raised eyebrows and the stare.

The chair crunched when Walter sat and met the Indian's eyes. He nodded and said, "No strings attached."

The Indian grabbed Stan Lowe's arm and pulled him closer. "Finally, I get money that mine, you stingy crook."

"What does that mean?" Stan asked.

Sammy rapped on the table and said to the Indian, "Do you want to explain, or should I tell him?"

The Indian stood, a cloth in hand. The wig was the first to come off, then the headband. The fake nose was wiped away with the smeared war paint. The figure stood tall and proud. "Now do you get it, you stingy lowlife?"

Stan Lowe was taken aback by the abrupt change in the Indian's facade.

"Why, it's a woman," someone said.

Stan Lowe cringed in disbelief. "My ex-wife? Grace, is that you?"

"No, it's Tonto," she said sarcastically. "You and your lawyer here connived to leave me penniless after the divorce. You humiliated me. I deserved more, and now I got it. Fifty thousand from Mr. Lawyer Watts and $200,000 from you."

"But the bones?" Stan said.

"I buried the bones the night before, so they would be dug up the next day."

Sammy joined in. "And you were at the site, ready to run down to make sure they saw the bones."

Grace Landis glanced at Sammy. "Mr. Bright Boy figured it out, didn't you?"

The sudden emergence of Grace from her hidden identity had surprised the young detective. He figured he would have to unmask the villain. But he was glad in a way that Grace Landis came forward on her own. His research in the last couple of days indicated that Grace Lowe got a raw deal in her divorce from her husband Stan Lowe. There were no children involved, and she was left with minimal income. Her only favorable option was to return to her nursing job and revert to her maiden name, Landis.

While all eyes were on Sammy, he explained his understanding of the case. "I first suspected Grace as the mystery 'man' when Brian and I were at your house, Mr. Hoover. You reminded me that Grace saw the bones from the sidewalk. The sidewalk was at least 100 feet away. At that distance, it would take a camera with a zoom lens to see bones mixed with dirt."

Grace flicked her eyebrows but said nothing.

"Grace, you faked your own abduction to make yourself look like a victim. When you came to Brian and me from the police station, you said you were abducted that morning in the parking lot at the hospital. Yet you were wearing a blouse and jeans. If you were really dressed for work, you would have been wearing your nurse's uniform. Also, you told us that Detective Phillips had not mentioned to you about Brian being abducted. Yet, you mentioned that he, like you, was abandoned on Gibbons Road. Only the person responsible would have known that Brian was 'dropped off' on Gibbons Road."

Grace cast her eyes at Stan. "My ex-husband didn't marry me for my brains. He kept reminding me of that fact—every day."

Sammy continued. "At the North Museum, I saw a name on the volunteer list. *Grace Lowe.* I wondered if it might be you before your divorce. Mr. Lowe, you said you were recently divorced." Sammy twisted toward Walter Watts. "And Mr. Watts, you are a divorce lawyer. I checked the Internet. Grace Lowe's maiden name was Landis. Putting those facts together gave me the motive for this whole Indian bones' scenario. *Revenge.*"

Tom Boyer asked, "Who were the men who attacked me?"

Grace looked at the lawyer. "Still no strings attached?"

Walter Watts made no attempt to glance at Stan Lowe before answering. "Oh, no, you don't get away with that. The men are answerable for their crimes. That is, if Tom Boyer and Brian Helm want to file charges."

Brian glanced at Sammy for an indication of how to answer. A slight head shake pleased Brian, who didn't want to cause trouble for anyone. "No," Brian said. "Actually, as I look back, it was an interesting experience."

Everyone looked at Tom.

"I figure I was punished for my silence involving the bones," Tom said, and then he added with a grin,

"I won't file charges if you give me a baseball bat and two minutes with those men."

"The two men were my brothers," Grace said. "Things did get a little out of hand. I told them to scare you a bit so you wouldn't report the bones."

"What you are saying doesn't make sense," Sammy said. "You planted the bones to be discovered to shut down the construction site. You did this as revenge against your ex-husband. Next, you didn't want Tom Boyer to report the bones. Later, you tell Brian to deliver the bones to you. What was that all about?"

"When Tom and Harry didn't report the bones, they ruined my revenge against this jerk," Grace said, thrusting her elbow toward her ex-husband. "So I decided to get the money I should have gotten in the divorce. I blackmailed my ex-husband and his lawyer. If Tom had reported the bones, that would kill my chances at blackmail."

"But why Brian?"

"I followed your girlfriend from your house to Harry Hoover's house. I waited outside the window and saw Harry bring the bones for her to photograph. I followed the girl back to your house. I figured she told you and Brian that Harry had the bones. Since these two wouldn't pay me the money I deserved, I wanted the bones back. I thought with the bones in my possession, I had leverage to force these two lump heads to pay up. I wanted you two to get the bones for me, so I called my brothers. I figured if I scared Brian with my Indian act, he and you would get the bones. But you didn't, so my brothers broke into Harry Hoover's house and took them. And the rest you know. When they offered me a deal with no questions asked, I finally got what I wanted. Thanks to you and Brian."

"You should thank yourself for not rubbing away all the writing on the bone. If you had eliminated all the markings, who knows how this case would have ended?"

Two men entered the conference room. They looked like two actors on a stage without a script. Brian, who no one saw leave the room, stood beside them.

"Get in there, both of you," Brian said. "I found these two outside in a white car. They said they were waiting for their sister."

Tom glared at the men.

"Are you okay, Grace?" one brother asked.

Grace Landis smiled, added her dirty cloth, Indian wig, and headband to the moneybag, and walked past her brothers to the door. "Let's go home," she said. "I got what I came for."

Sammy saw Harry Hoover and Tom Boyer hustle out the door, followed by Stan Lowe. Sammy smiled and took a deep breath. They were glad the Indian bones' episode was over, and so was he. However, one unexplained incident remained.

Sammy went over to Walter Watts' chair. He half-sat on the table, faced him, and said, "Everything went well."

Walter looked up at Sammy. "Yeah, for you. I'm out $50,000."

"You're out more than that."

"How is that?"

"What did it cost you to arrange for the purse snatching act in California?"

"You know about that?"

"You're the only one who had the knowledge of what was happening in California. The boss out there probably told you that Mr. Helm was considering returning to Lancaster. You were afraid he'd come back, and as a result, the existence of the bones would be revealed. So what did it cost you?"

Walter lowered his head. "Three thousand dollars. A part-time actor and his wife staged it for $3,000."

"So you're out $53,000. Your client, Stan Lowe, seemed satisfied with the results. That should endear him to you and your law firm." Sammy slid from the table and stood. "Fifty-three thousand dollars is a cheap price to pay for his continued business."

Walter Watts considered Sammy's comment. "Looking at it that way, it makes sense."

Brian walked in with Alison Mallin and smacked his hands together. "That takes care of another case. Right, Sammy? I told Mrs. Mallin we had the Indian bones for her."

"I'm very concerned," Alison said. "Grace went to the restroom a half hour ago and never came back. Did I miss something in here?"

Sammy scooped the bones from the table and handed them to Alison. "Thank you for your patience. And, no, you didn't miss a thing. I'd say everyone got what they deserved."

Chapter Twenty-five

The next morning, Brian came running up the steps to the bedroom. "It's not 9 o'clock yet. Right, Sammy?" he said out of breath and flopping back on the bed.

Sammy looked up from his desk and said, "I hope you brushed your teeth and used mouthwash this morning."

Brian lifted his head. "Why? What's that mean?"

Sammy smiled. "The way you're breathing, I wouldn't want the ceiling to get covered with germs."

"Hey, I want you to know that my hygiene is as high as it can get. Oh, my father said to thank you for what we did last night."

"Your father can relax now. His promise to Tom Boyer was kept, and everything was resolved. As it turned out, the Indian bones came from the North Museum and not from the construction site. So your father is home free.

Brian frowned at the ceiling. "Sammy, did my father do the right thing?"

Sammy pushed his pen and paper aside on his desk. He sat back and glanced up at the same ceiling that Brian consulted. "Brian, we all have to live with the choices we make in life. The people in this case are all decent. They just got tangled up in their values."

"Do I have values, Sammy?"

"We all have values. They have to do with our beliefs. We feel certain ways about things that concern us."

"How do I know what my values are? I just do stuff."

"That's just it, Brian. We don't really know what our values are until we are in a position to act upon them. Everyone in our recent case had a chance to test his or her values. Hopefully, each will learn from the experience."

"You know, Sammy, no other house in the world has a ceiling like your bedroom. This ceiling is discolored. It has cracks and spider webs. But, you know, this ceiling is unique because it's ours."

"The ceiling is like our friendship, Brian," Sammy said.

Brian thought for a moment. "Is that another metaphor, Sammy?"

Sammy nodded. "Yes, I believe it is."

"Good, I like that," Brian said, crossing his arms over his chest and smiling at the ceiling.

The End